Love Along the Lakeshore: A Saugatuck Summer

Joan Donaldson

Love Along the Lakeshore: A Saugatuck Summer

For Eileen
Thank you for your encouragement

By
Joan Donaldson

Copyright © 2021 by Joan Donaldson.

All rights reserved.

Created in digital format in the United States of America. No part of this book may be used or reproduced in any manner whatsoever without written permission of the author except in the case of brief quotations in blog posts and articles and in reviews.

A Saugatuck Summer except in a few instances, names, characters, places, and incidents are the products of the author's imagination or are used fictitiously. Where familiar places in Michigan are mentioned, it is in a completely fictitious manner.

Description

When wealthy Ginny Madden encounters a rugged fruit farmer, Andrew McBride, she questions her future role of marrying a Chicago elite as prescribed by her parents. It's 1915 in the art colony of Saugatuck, Michigan, and Ginny prefers sketching with other artists, helping on Andrew's farm, and cooking. Andrew longs to nurture a second chance at love with Ginny.

Weary of her parents' expectations to marry the man of their choice and enter the prestige and power of Chicago's society, Ginny Madden chooses a different path. When the family's summer cook suddenly cancels, Ginny assumes and revels in the responsibilities of cooking at their Lake Michigan cottage. Needing advice from lighting a fire to baking biscuits, Ginny bonds with Andrew McBride and his mother and they instruct her in homemaking skills. She also offers to help at certain farm jobs and comes to love both the farmer and his orchards. But her parents reject her romance with Andrew and insist upon a courtship with a family friend who is determined to marry Ginny. Fueled by her passion for the suffragist movement and her friendship with a female art student, Ginny grows in confidence and dreams. She flees from her parent's choices and into Andrew's arms who encourages her newfound identity. Happily wed, they cultivate their love and farm on Lake Michigan's shoreline.

Praise and Awards

First place winner of the Pencraft 2018 Award for Romantic Suspense

Hearts of Mercy

2010 Friends of American Writers Award for Outstanding Young Adult Novel,

On Viney's Mountain

"Viney and her mountain ridge are beautifully realized...readers will come to love feisty Viney and cheer her on." Kirkus Review for *On Viney's Mountain*.

"A captivating tale about father-daughter relationships, personal independence, and second chances." Kirkus Review for *Hearts of Mercy*.

"An excellent heroine, an intriguing historical hook, and a wonderful sense of character." Indie Reader. Indie Reader selected *Hearts of Mercy* as an IndieReader approved book and featured it as one of their books of the month in their newsletter.

"*Hearts of Mercy* is the perfect book to cuddle up with on a rainy day." Authors Reading.

Table of Contents

Chapter One	1
Chapter Two	15
Chapter Three	31
Chapter Four	45
Chapter Five	65
Chapter Six	81
Chapter seven	101
Chapter Eight	121
Chapter Nine	141
Chapter Ten	159
Chapter Eleven	171

Chapter Twelve	195
Chapter Thirteen	223
Chapter Fourteen	241
Epilogue	257

Chapter One

The faint sound of the train whistle rippled down the Kalamazoo River as Ginny Madden settled into her seat on the small steamer. Trunks, carpet bags, a barrel of flour, a crate filled with bags of coffee, and a wheel of cheese occupied the space on the narrow deck. A black plume billowed from the smokestack, and the vessel pulled away from the dock at New Richmond aiming for the center of the river. In his traveling suit and shiny shoes, Ginny's father chatted with the river pilot dressed in a blue chambray shirt, denim overalls, and thick-soled boots. The pilot sported a wide brimmed straw hat to protect his face, but a straw boater graced her father's head. As a business owner, he didn't worry about the sun, because he took his constitutionals in the evening with Ginny's mother holding his arm. They would stroll through Oak Park greeting folks until they circled back home.

In the slanted sunlight, Ginny's mother napped in a chair. Smudges of soot stained the hem of her white dress, and a little gold watch pinned to the bodice sparkled. She had donned a large hat decorated with pink silk roses to cover her honey blonde hair and the flowers matched her rosy cheeks. Her mother had organized every detail for their summer holiday while her father paid for their tickets and closed his office for three months.

Trailing her fingers into the river, Ginny wanted to stoke the belly of the steamer and increase its speed so they could shorten their trip. The Kalamazoo twisted and curved around wooded bluffs, cleared fields planted to peach orchards, and small homesteads where roosters crowed. A large dog ran down to the edge of the river barking at the boat. After the hectic streets of Chicago, Ginny relished the call of an Indigo Bunting from nearby oak trees. She marveled as a Great Blue Heron rose from its fishing spot, flapping its giant wings as it flew downstream. The rays of the evening sun shimmered on rippling water. What would it be like to experience all four seasons along the lakeshore and to gaze out from the top of a dune at the snowy landscape?

The Kalamazoo widened into an estuary where eagles perched near their nests and swans floated by beds of cat tails. A man fishing from a rowboat lifted his hat as their vessel passed him leaving a fan-shaped wake. Ginny leaned forward as they sailed into Silver Lake. The low wooden buildings of the basket factory, tannery and sawmill lined the shore near Douglas. The little steamer chugged onward to the chain ferry, where the pilot reduced their speed and stopped at a narrow dock. He threw a thick rope and a young man tied it to a piling.

"Here you be." The boatman offered his hand to Mrs. Madden and helped her onto the dock while the other man began to unload the baggage carrying it to a waiting wagon.

After tipping the boatman, Mr. Madden gathered two carpet bags. "You're young Andrew McBride, correct?"

"Yes, sir. My father died last October." Andrew hauled a crate off the steamer.

"I'm sorry to hear that. A good man, he was."

"Thank you, sir." Andrew shoved the crate further up into the wagon bed and returned for the flour barrel.

Ginny appreciated how Andrew's broad shoulders stretched his muslin work shirt and his black braces. A patch covered one knee of the wool trousers that he had stuffed into leather work boots. His dark-brown hair stuck out from beneath a worn slouch hat and his gray blue eyes flickered over her.

From beneath her wide-brimmed hat, she smiled, and his grin brought a dimple to his chin. Yet, despite the flash of his teeth, a sadness lingered about Andrew's expression. But hadn't the man recently buried his father? He was in mourning, and the passage of the months would bring healing to his heart. Ginny studied his hands but saw no wedding ring.

After depositing her basket and small carpet bag, Ginny climbed into the back of the wagon, squeezing through the narrow spaces between the supplies, taking care not to catch her frock on a protruding nail. She wore her favorite summer dress sprinkled with blue forget-me-nots, tied at the waist with a pink ribbon sash. While their hired cook would visit the general store throughout the summer, her mother preferred to stock a well-stocked pantry that included her favorite coffee beans. Ginny began to unlace her boots so her feet would be ready to race down the beach.

"Ginny, come join us. It's not proper for you to ride there." Mrs. Madden frowned.

"And where would you have me sit? You and Papa will need to be on the seat with Mr. McBride." Ginny lifted her palms. "Being the youngest, I might as well ride here."

"Leave her be," Mr. Madden said. "It's a short ride and we're at the Lake."

Mrs. Madden shook her head. "That will work for tonight, but she's eighteen-years-old and needs to think about her appearances and behavior."

Ginny cringed. The lack of formal attire and corsets were the best parts of living on the lakeshore for three months, along with a daily swim. Would her mother take that away from her? Mr. McBride's countenance showed no emotions as he helped Mrs. Madden on to the wagon seat. But when he turned and faced Ginny, he raised one eyebrow as he untied the reins from a hitching post and sat down. She nodded and resumed removing her shoes and then her stockings. Why hadn't she noticed Andrew before? She had come to the Lake for the past fifteen years, but his father had met them with this same wagon and team of horses.

***

Andrew McBride clucked to the horses and they trudged along the road edging the river. He shouldn't have shown any emotions to Miss Madden. After all, he was a married man; at least legally, he was still married to Nancy. From the riverbank, the girl's strawberry blonde hair had drawn his gaze, like the clouds at sunset floating across a pearl-blue western sky. What would such hair feel like brushing his neck? He tamped down such longings and focused on the road and Mr. Madden's questions.

"Yes, sir, I was the only boy in the family and am taking over the farm. My sisters are married and live on the other side of the state. Yes, I am married, but after the death of our baby, my wife moved back home for a few months."

No need to shout out the painful details of how a few months had extended into a year, and despite his pleading, Nancy refused to leave Grand Rapids. And no, he wasn't going to sell the farm, move to the city, and work in a furniture factory. From the corner of his eye, Andrew noticed how Miss Madden had positioned herself so she could listen to his answers.

"How are the crops this year?" Mr. Madden asked.

"So far, the peaches escaped a late frost, and we should start picking strawberries in a week. We need a soaking rain but want to avoid any hailstorms." Andrew tugged on the reins and the team plodded up the steep dune and reached the top of the ridge. The first music of the waves greeted the travelers.

"Almost there," Mrs. Madden chimed in. "I hope the cook aired the cottage. It can be so musty after being closed up for the winter."

"She's Dutch. I'm sure the cottage will be clean and tidy." Mr. Madden patted his wife's arm.

"Whoa." Andrew pulled on the reins stopping at the crest of a dune. Although he had been born on the lakeshore and had never spent a night away from Lake Michigan, her waves still bewitched him. This evening, the sun had turned them into molten brass and the western sky blazed orange. A few months into his marriage, Andrew had realized how he loved the lake more than Nancy, more than his farm, more than his life. The Lake was his mistress, and he was her servant.

On the slope nestled between a few oak saplings squatted three cottages sided with brown shingles. Andrew hopped down and extended a hand to Mrs. Madden while her husband also jumped off the wagon. A blur flashed by as Miss Madden streaked over a path descending the dune and leapt onto the beach. That young lady was unlike any of the Chicago women Andrew had met.

***

Ginny ran into the lips of the waves, squealing as the cold water rushed up her calves. She loved every drop of lake water. Every wave slapping the shore. Every breeze tossing her hair. For nine months, she had mooned staring east over Chicago's harbor. She inhaled, feeling her muscles relax and her stiff neck soften. She wouldn't wear shoes except on Sunday. And if she were alone, Ginny would have turned cartwheels down the beach as she had as a ten-year-old.

From the top of the dune, her parents quarreled. Her mother's panicked voice rose while her father tried to calm her. Andrew continued to unload supplies and Ginny wondered if she should help him, or if her mother would object? Yet whatever had irritated Mother might keep her distracted for a while. Ginny climbed the dune, stepped to the wagon, and picked up her basket and carpetbag.

"I can carry those things, Miss Madden." Andrew reached for her luggage. "That's what I was hired to do." He had unbuttoned his cuffs and rolled up his sleeves.

"Oh, thank you, these aren't heavy." Ginny enjoyed the thatch of dark hair exposed on Andrew's forearms. Most of the young men who attended the dinner parties and balls couldn't have lifted any of the crates filled with groceries. A few had enough muscles to hit a tennis ball or to ice skate, but none understood manual labor. The teamsters who delivered coal lacked Andrew's social graces and patient attitude. In fact, when she spied the teamsters' wagons, she avoided strolling in the gardens.

"What are we going to do?!" Mrs. Madden stood close to the back door as Andrew entered with a crate filled with potatoes. "No one even took down the window covers."

"There might be a hammer somewhere." Mr. Madden scratched his neck.

"Is there something amiss, sir?" Andrew asked as he marched down the porch steps.

"Yes, very much so. We found a note that the Dutch widow took a different position near Zeeland so she could be closer to her mother and she also didn't arrange for a fellow to remove the boards covering the windows. He was supposed to air out the cottage and leave a fire in the fireplace for us."

Ginny pried her fingers underneath one of the boards but couldn't budge it. Her mother looked as if she would faint. All her organizing had not foreseen these challenges. Somehow, they would manage the coverings, but what would they do if they couldn't find a cook? Perhaps she could convince her mother to allow her to claim the kitchen.

Andrew withdrew a gold pocket watch. "I can stay a bit longer and help. Do you have a hammer?"

"There's a shed beneath the cottage with tools in it."

"But what about a cook? She was to clean, also." Mrs. Madden wiped her forehead with a lace edged hanky. "Mr. McBride, do you know of anyone who could cook for us?"

"Not at the moment. Most visitors stay at the boarding houses. But I can ask around."

"I'll cook," Ginny said. "I've watched Mrs. Cooley and helped a little. Tonight, we can eat the leftovers from our picnic lunch."

Mrs. Madden frowned. "I suppose you want to wash the dishes and sweep the floor, too?"

"Why not? Call it a summer adventure. Who knows, one day I may need to know those things." Ginny swung her hat by its ribbons. Cooks and scullery maids could go barefoot, and she had liked wearing one of Mrs. Cooley's aprons. She should have packed an apron to cover her dresses. Perhaps the last cook had left one in the pantry. Mostly, she had helped scramble eggs and had baked cookies with Mrs. Cooley, but surely, she could remember how to make potato soup.

Shaking her head, her mother rubbed her temples. "I suppose we could humor you for a few days. But Charles, you must wire Chicago and see if one of our friends could lend us a maid who can cook. What a pity that Mrs. Cooley is helping her daughter this summer."

"Perhaps for us, but I'm sure with four children and a new baby, her daughter appreciates the assistance," Ginny said. "We'll manage without her."

"Let me find a hammer." Mr. Madden unlocked the door to the shed.

***

Andrew wiped his forehead with a blue bandana. He didn't want to meddle but figured the lass might need some help in the kitchen. "Maybe my mother could loan Miss Madden her cookbook or write down some of her favorite recipes."

Ginny Madden may dress with ruffles and ribbons, but she displayed the spunk of an immigrant. From her expression, she looked forward to keeping house. Hopefully, Miss Madden had watched her cook start a fire in their wood stove and could chop her own kindling. He glanced at the small wood pile. They would need more within a week.

"Here." Mr. Madden offered a hammer. "I dragged out a ladder, too."

"Good. Why don't you tackle the windows closer to the ground and I'll take care of the higher ones?" Andrew steadied the ladder against the cottage, climbed up, pulled out the nails, and removed the large boards.

The window sash shot up and Ginny propped it open with a stick. "I thought I'd follow you and open the windows." She stuck her head outside. "Sweet Joseph, it smells so good. Don't you love the scent of pine needles?"

Her curls bounced around her cheeks and Andrew relished the way she shook them out of her eyes. He had to remember to ask his mother about loaning her stained book of *Good Housekeeping*, as Ginny might also need the additional advice about homemaking. Her soft hands testified to a life that had escaped manual labor. She looked at him to answer her question.

"Yes, I love the scent of pine needles. Sometimes in the fall, I toss pinecones into our fireplace so we can smell their fragrance." Why had he offered that information? Why did he think this city girl would be interested?

Andrew moved the ladder and continued taking down boards. One-by-one, Ginny opened the windows and paused to stare at the Lake or up at the sky. She commented on the size of the waves or a seagull flying over. After months of living with his silent mother, Andrew's tongue awoke.

"How many years have you come here?" He popped out a nail.

"Papa and his friends built these three cottages between 1897 and 1899. One each summer, but I don't remember much because I was only three."

"Why did they choose Saugatuck?" Andrew let a board drop to the earth. Before he departed, he would have to stack and store them in the shed.

"It's close to Chicago. We can ride the Interurban to New Richmond. Because it's beautiful here."

"Yes, it is." Between the majesty of Lake Michigan and the fertile soil for growing peaches, Saugatuck was the perfect place for him. But it had not been for his wife.

Chapter Two

In the morning twilight, Ginny struck another match, and held it against the crumpled newspaper. It flared but didn't ignite the log sitting on top of it. At this rate she would burn through *The Chicago Tribune* before a single egg had cooked. Why hadn't she paid attention to how Mrs. Cooley lit a fire? Because she hadn't entered the kitchen until after eating a fine breakfast of lemon muffins, fried eggs with bacon or sausage and plenty of tea. What magical tricks did their Irish cook possess?

Closing her eyes, Ginny leaned back with her palms on the floorboards and cherished the purring waves and the silver call of a wood thrush. She conjured an image of the stove back in Chicago. A wood box sat to the left of the firebox, along with a stack of newspapers. Wasn't there a short basket with twigs? No, they had been small, thin sticks. Where could she find some of those? Wait, there had been a hatchet in the wood box. Perhaps Mrs. Cooley had sliced a log into kindling. Out on the attached porch,

Ginny spied a hatchet stored in one corner. She wiped off the cobwebs and took it to the wood pile.

Standing a log on end, Ginny slammed down the hatchet, but it bounced off the wood. Raising her arm, she smashed it down but missed the log. The blade sank into the sand near her big toe. She yelped and step back.

"That's why I wear boots when splitting wood or kindling." Andrew walked down the sandy path and held out a stained cookbook. "I thought you might need this."

"Thank you. What I need is a fire to magically appear in the cook stove." Her mother would scream if she emerged and saw Ginny barefoot, with her hair down, talking to a man. While Andrew wasn't from society, he was still a male. In fact, he was more of a male than any man she had met.

"Allow me, please. Why don't you gather some dry pine needles?" Andrew took a smaller log, set it on a low stump next to the woodpile and whittled off thin slices.

***

Andrew willed his eyes to focus on the log instead of roaming over Miss Madden's small toes. She had tucked her crisp white shirtwaist into a navy-blue skirt. Holding the edges of her apron, she dropped handfuls of pine needles into it. When he finished splitting the kindling, Andrew scooped it up and walked into the kitchen that occupied a room partitioned off from the main section of the cottage.

This Atlantic Queen stove had only four lids as opposed to his mother's six lid model. Andrew pulled a lever. "This is the draft. See how it says open and closed on the lever? You open it when you want to start the stove and close it once the fire is going well. Then the heat is transferred to the oven."

He squatted, crumpled up a couple of sheets of newspaper, and stuffed them into the firebox. "Please bring me the pine needles."

Ginny scooped up some and placed them in his palm. Andrew longed to thread his fingers through hers, but instead he scattered the needles over the newspaper. He arranged the thin kindling and lit the paper.

"You have to start with the needles because the pitch in them will help ignite the kindling and once it catches on fire, then add a couple of smallish logs. Once they are burning, then you can stick in the bigger ones."

"How long before the oven heats up? I was going to bake muffins."

"It depends on the type of wood. Sassafras is good for a fast fire, but you want oak to heat the oven." Andrew slid his gaze away from the sprinkling of freckles like fairy dust on her nose.

"How do you know all this stuff?" Ginny gazed up at him.

"I grew up learning it." Andrew shrugged and looked out the window. He was married and shouldn't give in to the temptation to drink in her hazel eyes. "This *Good Housekeeping Cookbook* has all sorts of homemaking information."

The voice of Mr. Madden rumbled from inside the cottage. Andrew had better skedaddle before this girl's parents found them together. After Nancy's father had discovered them tangled in the dunes near their cottage, the man had demanded a wedding date. Despite his daughter's protest that there was no imminent need to rush into marriage, they had wed a month later.

"If you need anything, come down to the farm." Andrew pushed open the screen door.

The half-mile walk allowed him to clear his mind of Ginny's trim waist and slim ankles. He listed today's jobs: thin peaches until noon, cut hay, and check for raccoon damage in the strawberry patch. The miserable creatures had eaten most of the pink berries and he needed to do something about them. While he didn't like trapping to control animals, either the raccoons departed, or he wouldn't harvest any strawberries. He had already promised to sell his berries to the Butler and Riverside Hotels, so he had to make good on his word.

Sitting at their kitchen table, his mother looked up from her cup of tea. "I milked. You said you'd only be gone a few minutes."

"Miss Madden needed a lesson on starting a fire." Andrew washed his hands, settle at his place, and bowed his head. While forking in eggs and fried potatoes, he pondered how his mother had cooked countless breakfasts for her children and husband. She had rarely complained except on the hottest of summer afternoons. Nancy could cook simple dishes, but she had no desire to learn how to bake biscuits and her loaves of bread could be used as door stoppers. Why did a wealthy woman want to cook while a farm wife who had needed to feed her husband would rather embroider pillowcases?

***

After opening all the windows, Ginny stoked the fire as the fragrance of bacon sizzling drifted from the kitchen. Today, she would read about making biscuits because from what she remembered, they baked faster than muffins. She scrambled the eggs and spooned them onto the platter with the waiting bacon. With her head held high, Ginny carried the platter to the small dining room that could open out to a screened in porch.

"Smells wonderful," Mr. Madden said. "Bravo. Your grandmother was a great baker so perhaps you take after her."

"I hope so." Ginny pulled out her chair.

Her mother sniffed. "Hopefully, you won't need to cook for long. Washing dishes will ruin your hands."

Ginny chewed a forkful of eggs. Why couldn't her mother give her a tiny compliment and appreciate her breakfast? If she hadn't offered to cook, who would have prepared this meal? Where would she find baking yeast? And milk? The cook had taken charge of buying milk, butter and eggs, plus fresh fruit. But where? She would ask Andrew.

Ginny grated a bar of soap and realized how she hadn't heated water for washing the dishes. The tea kettle still steamed, but it didn't hold enough water to clean every dish and glass. How did Mrs. Cooley and other housewives cook a meal and remember to heat water at the same time? Ginny couldn't image how most women performed these tasks while caring for a flock of children.

After working the pump by the sink to fill one dish pan with rinse water, Ginny dribbled some of the hot water into another pan with the soap flakes. She scrubbed and rinsed the china before tackling the frying pan. The stack of dishes drying on a towel shone in the sunshine. How satisfying it was to perform tasks necessary for survival.

But would she feel the same pride after a summer of housework? Ginny wanted to walk on the beach and search for lucky stones, as those wee round disks with a center hole were hard to find. She was threading them onto a long garland that she planned to drape around her room. Soon more summer visitors would arrive, and they would comb the beach while she swept the floor.

Lunchtime was only three hours away, what would she feed her parents? She flopped into a rocker on the little porch attached to the kitchen. Inside the cottage, her mother wrote letters while her father read *The Tribune* on the larger side porch. Back in Chicago, food appeared at mealtimes and while she might express delight over one dish and distain for another, she had never had to think about *what* to cook. Now, Ginny couldn't escape from planning the next meal.

Her mother cleared her throat. "You will ask around for a cook? I'm hoping that after a few days of this charade, Ginny will come to her senses."

"And if she doesn't?" Her father asked. "She's never been like you."

"More's the pity. Then I will plan a large dinner party, something to overwhelm her."

Her father fell silent and rustled his newspaper. Ginny pressed her lips together. *Thank you, Mama for warning me. How kind of you to want me to fail.* She hoped there was a section in *The Good Housekeeping Woman's Home Cookbook* about how to prepare and give a dinner party. But for now, what should she do about lunch? Milk. Her mother had complained about not having milk for her tea. She would go ask Andrew.

"I'm going to look for milk." Ginny called out to her parents and slammed the screen door. If they grew hungry, let them eat crackers and cheese.

Ginny headed south down the sandy two track road that ran along the top of the dune. Only a few small beech and maple trees grew because the hemlock trees had been cut down for the tanning factories. A fence surrounded a pasture where sheep grazed. Leaning over the fence, Ginny offered a hand, but the sheep ran to the far side of the paddock. Silly creatures, but their lambs were adorable, and Ginny wanted to snuggle one.

Lake Michigan was magnificent. The teal-blue waves sparkled and lapped against the base of the dune. A few rowboats with anglers dotted the scene and far out from shore a thin line of smoke testified of a steamer chugging towards Chicago. When she resided at their summer cottage, the city seemed a gray fantasy. The Lake, the dunes, this was reality. Walking onward, Ginny spied Andrew's wagon sitting outside a white farmhouse with green shutters. A red brick chimney rose from the center of a green shingled roof. She admired the vegetable garden growing east of the house and the row of hollyhocks planted by a bay window. Ginny knocked on the screen door and breathed in the fragrance of fresh bread.

Boots tapped across the wooden floor, and a woman wearing a dark purple dress and white apron approached Ginny. "Yes, how can I help you?" She opened the screen door and stepped out onto the small porch.

"Mrs. McBride?" The lady sported Andrew's dark hair and sky-blue eyes, but her face was more oval.

"Yes? Are you from last night's family?" Mrs. McBride asked.

"Yes. Andrew drove my family to our cottage. I was wondering if either you or Andrew could tell me where I could buy milk? Your bread smells heavenly. Is there a baker in Douglas?"

"I'm afraid not. Most of us bake our own bread, but later in July, Mrs. Lewis from Saugatuck takes orders from visitors."

"I'll starve by then." Ginny inhaled. "Yours smells wonderful. Does the grocery sell yeast?"

"Usually, he carries cakes of yeast. Andrew said you were learning to cook. Why don't you step in for a minute? I need to take some rolls out of the oven."

Ginny followed Mrs. McBride into a yellow kitchen with blue gingham curtains. A black round top cage hung from a pole and from it a yellow canary cheeped a few notes. A cup full of flour sat on the table next to a white pastry cloth where Mrs. McBride had begun to roll out a circle of pie dough. Sugar sparkled over pieces of chopped rhubarb filling a gray pottery bowl. Bending over, Mrs. McBride grasped the oven door with a potholder and withdrew a pan of golden rolls.

While the McBride kitchen was much humbler than the grand one back in Chicago, it exuded the same feelings of anticipation and promise. Wasn't it a wonder how a woman could combine flour and yeast and bring forth crusty loaves of bread? Or turn sugar and rhubarb into a tangy pie? Ginny wanted to learn it all. She wanted her kitchen to smell like this one.

"Here." Mrs. McBride scooped a tan glob of something into a small crock. "I use a sourdough starter for my rolls, then I don't need to buy yeast. Makes good pancakes and biscuits too."

"How do I use it?" Ginny stared at the bubbling mass.

"Later, I'll write out a few recipes. For now, you can have a loaf." Mrs. McBride placed the crock and bread into a basket. "We sell milk. But you need to bring your own bucket for it."

"Oh, I was hoping to buy some now."

"Come back after the evening chores." Mrs. McBride tucked a tea towel over the top of the basket.

"I'll save you some." Andrew popped through a back door and snitched a roll. "We milk at five. Don't worry if you can't find a bucket. We have a couple of small tin ones." He tossed a roll to Ginny. "You look famished."

The warm bun spoke to her, but Ginny waited until Andrew had escorted her out of the house and they stood on the porch. She bit into it, savoring the tangy taste. "Your mother is a fantastic baker. She should open a shop."

"She's too busy with the garden and helping on the farm." Andrew nodded at the large vegetable garden where peas climbed a trellis. "Soon it will be canning season."

"I'll be back, later." Ginny walked backwards. "Thanks again for the bread."

***

What an odd girl. Andrew loved her bare feet and the glimpse of her petticoat inching below the hem of her dress. She had forgotten to wear a hat, and he hoped the sun wouldn't burn her nose. He removed his hat and went to the kitchen sink to wash the peach fuzz off his face.

"Careful." With her hanky, Mrs. McBride wiped the sweat from her forehead. "Any plans to go to Douglas?" She pulled out her chair and sat down with Andrew.

"Not today. Why?" Andrew heaped chicken and dumplings on to his plate."

"Think I'll walk in and pick up our mail." Mrs. McBride scooped a forkful of peas.

"I'll be in the orchard."

Andrew groaned as he moved the ladder and checked that it was well balanced. He shouldn't have eaten that second slice of pie, but rhubarb was one of his favorites. Climbing to the top, he stuck his head through a gap in the leaves and picked off most of the peaches, leaving about ten inches between the little green balls. If it would rain soon, the peaches would grow plump and juicy, and the crop would bring a tidy sum. Hopefully enough to pay off their bank debt on the sheep pasture. Peach fuzz floated down his neck and through the opening in his shirt. Mixing with his sweat, the fuzz formed an itchy plaster against his body. He yearned to rip off his skin and stop the itching.

Think about something pleasant, he told himself. Another slice of pie? No, his belly spoke. All through lunch, his mother had urged him to take the Interurban to Grand Rapids and visit with Nancy. But shouldn't Nancy come home instead of him going to her? After all, she was the spouse who had left. As he moved the ladder to a different tree, the image of Ginny Madden's bare feet flashed across his mind.

Mrs. Madden had said Ginny was eighteen, but she seemed younger. The girl was as curious as a child, but her shape was womanly. He shouldn't have noticed, but he had admired not only her feet, but her strong calves, the swell of her bosom, her slender neck, and full pink lips. Leaning a bit too far, Andrew felt the ladder sway and he clutched a branch. That's what would happen if his mind lingered on Miss Madden. He tried to conjure Nancy's face, but her red eyes, tear-soaked cheeks, and shaking shoulders dominated the image. Maybe his mother was right, as she usually was, and he should make that trip. He should admit to his fear that Nancy would refuse to return with him and ask for a divorce. The word sounded ominous, and a divorce would taint him as a scoundrel. Folks would assume he was guilty of infidelity, and the way his thoughts wandered, he had stepped onto that road.

Hauling back his arm, Andrew threw a green peach as hard as he could at a fence post. The small ball ricocheted off the post and flew into the pasture where the cow grazed. Andrew attempted a second throw. He was not the type of man to cheat on his wife, but he was lonely. Building a fire and chatting with Ginny, he should call her Miss Madden, had ignited a simple desire to talk with a woman. To stroll along the boardwalk in Saugatuck with a female and buy her an ice cream soda. Certainly, he would love to slip beneath the sheets with Ginny, but that wouldn't heal the loneliness. Andrew scanned the orchard. Two more trees to thin in this row and then he would cool off in the Lake.

Chapter Three

After pulling her shirtwaist over her head, Ginny unfastened the waistband of her skirt and it slid to the floor, along with her petticoat. She stepped out of her drawers and into the navy-blue bloomers and slipped on the short dress with a sailor's collar. Ginny would wear the mobcap while in view of the cottage but would toss it as soon as she jumped in the Lake. From age three, Ginny had loved swimming and frolicking in the waves, but today she yearned to cool off her flushed skin. Between the walk home under the noon sun and the hot cook stove, her body had never experienced such throbbing heat. She grabbed a towel and pushed open the screen door.

A few white sails dotted the open water and a mother walked along the shore with her young son and daughter. The children ran ahead of their mother and splashed each other. What would her childhood have been like if she had had some siblings? Would a brother have protected or tormented her? A sister could have been a friend, or she might have criticized Ginny's behaviors. She leapt from the edge of the low dune, dashed across the hot sand, and threw down her towel and cap.

Arms outstretched, Ginny dove into the two-foot wave and gasped. The bite of winter lingered in the water and sucked the air from her lungs. Rising from the waves, she swept the hair from her face and flopped backwards. Let the waves slap her rear end. Let the Lake wash away her sweat and refresh her muscles. Closing her eyes, Ginny floated as the waves rolled her towards the shore and placed her on the tiny gravel edging the beach. If she remained here, sand would sift into her bloomers and that would be unpleasant. Ginny jumped up and plunged in once again.

When gooseflesh prickled her chilled body, Ginny wandered south searching the sand for tiny gray lucky stones. Over the years, she had found a dozen with a star as the center hole, but most of the disks sported a simple circle. The extra lucky ones with the stars she had stored in a little tin that had held violet candies. The others graced a six-foot garland she had draped on one wall of her room. If the children spending a holiday at the Lake would concentrate on building sandcastles, she would fill another chain by the end of the summer. She glanced up and blushed.

Without a shirt, Andrew stood in the Lake, scrubbing himself with a bar of soap. Dark hair thatched his chest and forearms; his wet pants pasted to his firm thighs. His shoulder muscles rippled as Andrew scooped up handfuls of water and doused his face. He lathered his chest and sank below the waves.

Ginny had never seen a man wearing so few clothes. Most men wore long woolen bathing suits and when wet, the fabric revealed a man's basic shape. Should she say something when Andrew surfaced? Or should she discretely hasten home? Andrew was married and she should depart, but the flash of his arms swimming away stilled her feet. Such grace and strength flowed from each stroke propelling him to the sandbar.

***

Planting his feet in the sand, Andrew rose and shook the hair out of his eyes. Nothing cooled off a fellow like a good swim and it removed the misery of peach fuzz. He loved growing peaches, but Andrew would be relieved when he had finished thinning his trees. Glancing down the shoreline, he spied Ginny and groaned.

How long had she watched him? Had she liked what she had seen? *Stop it!* He enjoyed how her wet bloomers hugged her rear end and the sailor top clung to her bosom. Even from a distance, her exposed calves and bare arms drew his eyes. He was grateful for the water separating him from her. She waved and he returned it. Turning around, Ginny walked back towards her cottage. Andrew ducked beneath the waves, willing the Lake to chill his flesh.

Because desire blazed inside him, and he must extinguish it before mistakes happened. He refused to give Nancy a reason to divorce him. Or a reason for the church elders to knock on his door and ask questions about his conduct and soul. His mother was right. On Sunday, he would travel to Grand Rapids and confront Nancy. She needed to return with him and fulfill her duties as his wife. Andrew swam back to shore and gazed down the beach at the blurry image of a navy-blue swimsuit. Trudging up the dune, he looked forward to when Ginny would come for her pail of milk.

After donning dry clothes, Andrew headed for the barn. The flock of goldfinches flew over his mother's garden, and a swallowtail butterfly flitted about a pink rose bush. Those roses combined with white ones had perfumed the front of the Congregational Church two years ago when he had wed Nancy. Thankfully, his father had witnessed the nuptials and had died shortly before Nancy had left him.

If their daughter had lived, would Nancy have stayed? Without his mother knowing, Andrew had written once and asked if he could visit, but a single word stared up at him from Nancy's reply. *No*. After her cool response, he had plunged himself into farm work, hauling manure from the stalls and fertilizing his trees. He had repaired crates and barrels, built a garden shed for his mother, and from plans he had bought, he had constructed a machine for spraying his trees. But a peach orchard could not replace a child or the warmth of a wife on a winter's night.

***

Climbing the path to the cottage, Ginny relished the breeze rustling the leaves and cooling the desire inside her. While she had danced and attended dinner parties with

Chicago's most wealthy young men, she had not experienced such heat in her belly. Those men were like a baker's bran muffin; uniform and tasteless yet considered good for a person. Ginny yearned for another of Mrs. McBride's sourdough rolls, tangy and salty. Did salty sweat edge Andrew's lips? Entering her room, Ginny pulled off her swimming garb and chose a dress with quarter-length sleeves and a rounded neck. The pale pink lawn added sparkle to her eyes and was a better choice for enduring the late afternoon heat. After greeting her mother and father, Ginny tied on an apron and plopped down in her rocker opening Mrs. McBride's book.

The spattered pages of the cookbook witnessed to years of trying out recipes. Mrs. McBride had penciled in comments on some: *One of Andrew's favorite. Mac didn't care for this. Loved at the church potluck.* Ginny would have to copy any that Andrew had enjoyed, but for the present, she needed a simple dish for their supper. Perhaps she could concoct an omelet with eggs, onions, and cheese. And biscuits! Ginny flipped the pages until she found a recipe for them. Although she had no milk, she would substitute water.

Following Andrew's instruction, Ginny lit a fire and stoked the stove. Thank goodness for the numerous windows that allowed the lake breeze to flow into the kitchen. She cut lard into a mixture of flour, salt, and baking soda until crumbles formed then she added the water and mixed the dough. Slipping the pan into the oven, Ginny straightened up and wanted to hug someone. Although cooking required planning and labor, she had never felt more pride in herself. For a flick of a butterfly's wing, she considered taking an offering of biscuits to Andrew's mother. Perhaps another time.

"Omelets for supper?" Her father unfolded his napkin and spread it over his lap.

"Perhaps such fare will prompt you to look for a cook." Mrs. Madden bowed her head, waiting for the blessing.

"Thank you, God for this food and for my adventurous daughter. Amen." Mr. Madden plucked a biscuit from a platter as Ginny handed him the butter dish. "A bit on the heavy side."

"Yes." In fact, the disks resembled the brown, flat stones spit up by the waves. The biscuits tasted like she had mixed beach sand into the dough. This evening, she would have to ask Mrs. McBride for some tips, and she needed to find out where to purchase butter and eggs.

As the screen door swished closed, Ginny raised her right arm and threw three biscuits into the dune grass. Perhaps a chipmunk would enjoy them more than her family. Ambling down the road, the cooing of a morning dove soothed her feelings. With some practice, she would learn how to make biscuits and other baked goods besides the cookies she had created with Mrs. Cooley. Ginny knocked on the McBride door, and Andrew stepped onto the porch.

"Let's go around to the back, the milk is cooling in our well house." Barefoot and hatless, Andrew swung a gallon tin pail as he walked along a sandy path to a small stone building half sunk into the earth.

"Your mother's garden is amazing. I love her peonies." Ginny bent over a fluffy pink blossom and inhaled the delicate scent. While a handy man in Chicago managed their smooth lawns and neat gardens, Ginny preferred the way Mrs. McBride's flowers wandered close to the paths, sometimes tumbling over it. A hummingbird zoomed over to a red hollyhock and drank its nectar. Whenever she had a home of her own, Ginny would insist that a corner of the garden be planted like this one.

"She's fond of flowers but has to spend most of her time in the vegetable garden." Stopping at a small stone building, Andrew opened a narrow door and stepped down into a cool room.

Ginny accepted Andrew's hand, and her shoulder brushed his as she jumped into the wellhouse. Careful, she warned herself as her cheeks flushed. Ginny wanted no part in causing further division between Andrew and his wife.

Two metal milk cans stood in a wooden tank filled with water. By twisting a valve, Andrew drained part of the tub, then worked a pump and cold water splashed into the trough. Condensation dripped from the rock walls and an earthy scent filled the small chamber. No spiders lurked on the wooden ceiling, and a broom in a corner explained their demise.

"Where did you find so many rocks? There aren't any on our beach." Should she tell him how she was collecting lucky stones, or would Andrew think her childish?

"Down at Pier Cove, a few miles south of here. Most of the time, I take my peaches to the ships docked at Saugatuck, but sometimes they fetch a better price at Pier Cove." Andrew hoisted a milk can and filled the tin pail.

"I've never been there. I suppose because we don't keep a horse and buggy." Ginny accepted the bucket. "Thank you. How much do I owe you? And does your mother sell eggs and butter?"

***

"Why don't we keep a tally of the milk and you can pay once a month for it. My mother only churns butter on Tuesdays and Fridays, and I'd be glad to save you a couple pounds. There's a basket of fresh eggs in the kitchen you can take now." Andrew offered Ginny his hand and assisted her over the wellhouse stoop.

He yearned to hold her slim fingers a few seconds longer, but instead released them. Hadn't the affair with Nancy started with lingering touches until they had collapsed between the dunes? How he wished that her family had rented a cottage near Ganges or Glenn and not along the Douglas shoreline. At nineteen, Andrew had known better, but the fire ripping through him had incinerated common sense. Nor had Nancy insisted that he stop. Instead, she had unbuttoned his shirt while he slipped down her bodice. Closing the narrow door, Andrew shook the thoughts from his mind, thankful that Ginny wandered in the vegetable garden.

"What are those?" She pointed at a round vegetable with numerous stalks poking up from its top.

"A kohlrabi. They do look odd, but they taste like cabbage." Andrew relished the curious expression on Ginny's face.

"Those are beans on the tipi things?" Ginny fingered a heart-shaped leaf.

"Yes, scarlet runner beans and lima beans. Let's go find those eggs."

His mother looked up from the kitchen table and raised her eyebrows. "Oh, hello Miss Madden. I just finished writing out a few recipes for the sourdough starter." She handed Ginny a few sheets of paper covered with precise penmanship.

"Thank you. We came for eggs." Ginny folded the papers and stuck them in her apron pocket.

"There's some in the pantry." Mrs. McBride wiped her pen. "On the third shelf on the right."

Andrew emerged with a small woven basket filled with brown eggs. "Is a dozen enough for now? We collect more every day." For a moment he wished Ginny could experience the pleasure of reaching for a warm just laid egg.

"That's great. Thank you." Ginny took the basket and headed for the back door.

"Why don't I walk you home as you've got a lot to carry." Opening the door, Andrew sensed his mother's frown and the concern in her eyes.

He carried the tin pail and basket, and they strolled down the two-track as the sun dipped closer to the horizon. Smooth as slate, the Lake shimmered and glistened as the first rays of the sunset lit the water. As seagulls flew along the lakeshore, they called their plaintive cry. Andrew nodded at Mr. Johnson as he drove by in his buggy. Ginny's skirt swished against his pant legs and he inhaled. Although they ambled in silence, this young woman was a bean plant sending tendrils that encircled his waist and climbed towards his heart.

Chapter Four

While his mother fussed about train schedules, Andrew straightened his necktie and slipped into the suitcoat that his father had worn to church every Sunday. The last time Andrew had donned the wool suit was when they had buried his father in the Douglas Cemetery. Why did he feel as if today might yield another funeral?

"Don't worry about the evening milking. Take your time with Nancy. Show her you care about her."

"Yes, mother." Andrew settled his straw boater on his head and hurried out the door.

The morning dew sparkled on the cut lawns and daisies smothering a nearby field. He considered picking Nancy a bouquet, but the flowers would wilt by the time he reached Grand Rapids. At the chain ferry, Andrew rang the bell and the ferryman returned from the Saugatuck side of the Kalamazoo River. Andrew paid the fee. The chain rattled as the man cranked, and the ferry moved across the swift current. A few ducks floated near the shore, hoping for breadcrumbs. Andrew leaned on the ferry railing, hearing his mother reminding him how this trip could repair his marriage. But did he want to heal it?

Outside the Butler Hotel, a small crowd of men in linen suits, women in white lawn frocks and children dressed in their Sunday finest waited for the next train. Andrew purchased a ticket for forty-nine cents and joined the others, listening to their conversations.

"One of these days, folks will drive automobiles instead of taking the trains," one man said.

"Oh, I doubt it. How could the average man afford one of those noisy machines?" Another man commented.

"I see it!" A child shouted as the electric green train rumbled closer and stopped.

Andrew handed his ticket to the conductor and settled in car #28. Mothers stored picnic baskets under their seats and arranged their children to avoid bickering and pinching. Men unfolded newspapers and began to read. The train rolled out of Saugatuck and north towards Holland.

Every few miles, the train stopped at a small white booth located near the tracks and took on more passengers. The engine's wheels hummed along the rails that in places bordered a road lined with trees. A sign pointed to Castle Park, another resort catering to the wealthy from Chicago. Leaning back in his seat, Andrew studied the woods, open fields, and small farms until the train turned onto South Shore Drive and headed into Holland.

Only twice had Andrew ridden into the Dutch city to speak with a lawyer about his father's will. The farm provided most everything he and his mother needed other than a few grocery staples and hardware. Each spring the hardware owner ordered the sulfa chemicals to spray on his peach trees. Andrew hated Holland's busy streets, the closeness of the brick shops, and the houses sitting on small town lots. He would die if he had to live in a city where in the winter coal smoke hung over the town. Andrew stretched his legs as they reached the final stop on River Avenue where he would transfer to the train going to Grand Rapids.

Some of the exiting passengers hugged relatives and walked away from the station while others joined Andrew on the platform. Checking his watch, Andrew judged the next train would arrive in five minutes, unless an accident had occurred.

Now and then the newspapers reported about the interurban hitting a team and wagon or a car that attempted to cross the tracks but had misjudged how quickly the engine approached. While most trains traveled at forty miles per hour, sometimes the engineer accelerated the contraption to fifty-five miles per hour. Andrew gazed at the tracks running down Eighth Street. No one needed to move at such a high speed. A body couldn't absorb the landscape as houses, farms and rivers flashed by.

The air hummed as the interurban rumbled to the station and stopped. With the other assortment of travelers, Andrew stepped into one of the two coaches and claimed a seat by a window. Leaning against the wooden back, he closed his eyes and prayed this trip would be fruitful. The scent of lily of the valley moved down the aisle as a lady sought a seat. During the summer they had met, Nancy had worn that fragrance. For their wedding night, she had dabbed rose perfume on her neck and collar bones as he had pulled the pins from her hair. She had slid off his nightshirt as he unfastened the pearl buttons on her nightgown and lifted it over her head. Did Nancy ever think about those passionate moments they had shared?

At each little village, Zeeland, Forest Grove, Jamestown, the train paused allowing passengers to disembark or enter the coaches. Instead of English, many of the men and women spoke Dutch while their children chattered in either language. Andrew gazed at the rich black soil planted with rows of celery or onions and the many sheep grazing in pastures. Although the Dutch built odd, low barns with steep roofs, they tended tidy fields and thriving flocks. But the only fruit trees grew in the small orchards close to their homes to provide for their families.

When the train stopped in downtown Grand Rapids, Andrew walked up Wealthy and turned onto the street where Nancy's parents resided in a two-story brick house. Four cream-colored columns held the porch roof that doubled as a balcony, and two small dormer windows poked out of the main roof. They provided light to the tiny maids' rooms sectioned off from the attic. After their church wedding, Andrew had entered the stately home for the first time for their wedding reception. Standing beside Nancy and Mr. and Mrs. Phelps, Andrew had felt himself shrink each time he shook another soft hand. What madness had driven him to marry a woman from society? He needed to remind himself of this mistake whenever thoughts of Miss Madden popped up.

A maid in a black dress and white apron opened the door and stared. "Aren't you…?"

"Yes, I am Nancy's husband." Removing his hat, Andrew walked into the foyer.

"Who is it, Biddy?" Mrs. Phelps called from the parlor.

The dark wood paneling running down the hallway squeezed Andrew's lungs. Even the beige wallpaper covered with green ferns couldn't lighten the mood of the house. The Waterford crystal chandelier tinkled as he stepped through the parlor doorway.

"Good afternoon, Nancy, Mrs. Phelps." Andrew nodded his head but dared not walk farther into a space where he might not be welcome. At first their eyes displayed shock, but anger flooded Mrs. Phelps' expression.

"Good afternoon, Andrew. I wasn't aware that you had ask to call on us," Mrs. Phelps said.

Did he need a formal invitation to speak with his wife? Or had Mrs. Phelps drawn Nancy so far back into her old world that they had forgotten about him? Then blast it all, he and Nancy should divorce. Probably the family wanted to avoid the scandal, but who knew, being a divorcee might make Nancy more intriguing and desirable.

"I would like to speak with my wife, please. Perhaps we could visit in your gardens." Andrew looked into Nancy's eyes.

Sitting in a crisp white gown of eyelet lace, the bodice hugged Nancy's bosom and a blue sash set off her trim waist. From her tiny feet wearing silk slippers to her delicate wrists to her oval face framed by blonde hair, Nancy could have graced the cover of *Lady's Home Journal*. So why had her father demanded they marry? Because of the fear of an illegitimate child and how it would taint their reputation. The man had told his friends how Andrew was a peach Barron who owned hundreds of acres and sold thousands of baskets of peaches to the markets in Chicago. But when a baby arrived a year after the wedding, Mr. Phelps comprehended how Andrew had spoken the truth about his times with Nancy.

"Do you wish to go with him?" Mrs. Phelps took her daughter's hand as Nancy rose.

"Yes, for a little while."

Andrew and Nancy headed to the hall and waited for a maid to bring her blue hat smothered with pink silk roses and white feathers. After she had secured it with several hat pins, Nancy accepted his arm. Andrew smiled at his wife. Perhaps without her mother interrupting and bullying her daughter, they might have a decent conversation.

"The gardens are lovely," Andrew said as they strolled down a gravel path. A climbing red rose covered a white arbor with dozens of blossoms. A yellow swallowtail butterfly visited a blushing foxglove flower, and clumps of daisies bloomed close to the path.

"Yes." Nancy nodded making the feathers on her hat to sway.

What should he say next? Nancy was pale, but she had always shunned the sun and the outdoors. When he had suggested how she could help his mother weed in the vegetable garden, she had stated that he should hire someone for the task. Should he say something about their grief?

"I am sorry about the loss of our little daughter. Remember the doctor said that there was nothing we could have done to prevent her death." Andrew slipped off his hat and ran his fingers through his hair. "If you returned with me, we could try again."

Nancy shuddered and her shoulders shook as tears trickled down her cheeks. "That doctor was wrong. Living on that farm, breathing in your animal and chemical smells. They poisoned my baby."

Andrew stared at Nancy's reddening face. "But my mother birthed six children, and other farm wives have healthy babies." He had assumed fresh air and working in a garden was good for women in the family way. Why his mother had even picked peaches when expecting his youngest sister.

"I'm not one of those women." Nancy slumped onto a garden bench and sobbed.

Andrew slid next to her, and tried to hold her, but Nancy pushed him away and dabbed at her tears. He watched an ant carrying a leaf three times its size. How much longer could he carry the burden of their marriage? In the year they had lived together, he had realized how Nancy had rebelled against her parents by marrying him, a yokel from the lakeshore. Once the novelty had eroded, bitter words had surfaced, but he had hoped their child would revive their love. When that dream dissolved, Nancy had departed.

"Do you want a divorce?" Andrew whispered. Saying the word meant defeat, but how could he continue to lie about his wife when answering people's nosy questions.

"I couldn't face the shame." Nancy exploded into sobs.

"Do you assume I want people thinking I'm the culprit?" Andrew bit his lower lip. Shame! While Nancy could sequester herself in this fine brick house tended by servants, he had to walk into the post office where everyone knew him. For weeks, his ruined marriage would fuel the local gossips. Nancy's future wealth would insure her another suitor, selected and vetted by her mother.

***

"There." Mrs. Madden placed a stamp on the last small envelope. "If everyone invited attends, we should have a dozen guests. Now to select a menu."

"I thought I'd wait to figure out what to serve after we knew the total count." Ginny rubbed a fork with a rag and silver polish. She had never considered how eggs darkened silver. "And it would be good to wait and see what fruits and vegetables will be available at that week."

"Mrs. Cooley and I always determine the menu weeks before so she would have time to shop and prepare for the dinner." Mrs. Madden stood and gazed out the window. "If you insist upon cooking, then you must follow my directions. In late June, we should find fresh strawberries, garden peas and maybe new potatoes. We will serve a crown roast of pork and you can bake an angel food cake for strawberry shortcake." Mrs. Madden sniffed. "Is something burning?"

Ginny dropped the fork and raced into the kitchen. Hard boiled eggs hopped up and down in a sauce pan devoid of water. The bottom of the pan had turned black, and patches of dark gray splotches decorated the eggshells. Snatching a potholder, Ginny grabbed the pan, stuck it under the pump and worked the handle. If she couldn't manage to hard-boil eggs, how could she roast anything? And didn't a crown roast wear those silly paper decorations on the bones sticking out of the meat? Poor hog, he had to die to wear crowns. Where on the lakeshore could she find a butcher who could sell her that cut of pork?

Ginny carried the pot outside and walked to where a cluster of honeysuckle bushes edged the road. One-by-one, she tossed the eggs into the underbrush. She contemplated throwing away the pot, but come morning, she would need to cook oatmeal in it. Hadn't she read somewhere that pioneers scrubbed their pans with dirt? Bending down, she scooped in a handful of sand and spied familiar boots trudging down the road.

Shoulders slumped. His eyes gazed at his feet as Andrew plodded homeward. What had happened to make him so glum? Where had he gone dressed in a suit? Had a horse died and that's why he had walked to the village? When Andrew looked up, Ginny strolled over to him.

Although she wanted to take his hand and console him, Ginny only touched his shoulder. "Is something amiss?"

"Yes." Andrew removed his hat. "Something has been amiss for a year now, and I see no way to repair it."

Ginny froze. Andrew spoke of his marriage. "Did you go…?" A weariness lingered in Andrew's eyes, a fatigue of his soul.

"Yes. Rather pointless, really." Andrew stared at the Lake. "I should have stayed home and read a book."

"Perhaps over time, she will reconsider her response." What sort of woman would throw away a fine man like Andrew? Any person would grieve the death of a child, but how much better his wife would feel if she grieved with Andrew.

"I rather doubt it. I best head home." Andrew placed his hat on his head and walked away. Dust puffed with each of his steps and coated the hem of his pants.

While a cardinal chipped at his evening song, Ginny watched Andrew's back until he rounded a bend in the road. There must be something proper and respectable she could do to lighten his spirits, but her mother would not offer advice for someone beneath her station. Hopefully, Mrs. McBride could provide solace for her son.

Ginny returned to the kitchen, scrubbed the pot until the bottom shone and hung it on the wall above the cook stove. Flinging her apron over the little rocker, she ran down to the beach. How many days had she gone bare foot? Ten or twelve? Once she had worn her shoes when leaving the cottage but had hid them behind the wood pile before walking to the McBride Farm. She had visited the farm almost every day except Wednesday and today, Sunday. Each time, Mrs. McBride had answered baking and homemaking questions and offered suggestions about meal preparations. If the woman didn't have such an abundant flower garden, Ginny would have bought her a bouquet.

Ambling north along the beach, Ginny focused on the narrow area where the waves slapped the sand and sucked back the tiny pebbles. Thin mares' tails clouds rippled in the west, turning the sunset into apricot and rose. She reached down and picked up a small gray stone with a hole in its center. Her first lucky stone for the season. She would give it to Andrew as a sign of hope.

***

From the small woods by the edge of the pasture, floated the flute-like call of a wood thrush. Andrew stripped the last squirts of milk from Daisy and released her from the stanchion so she could go out and graze. Running feet approached the barn and a boy materialized out of the morning fog.

"Are you Mr. McBride?" The boy held a telegram.

At first, Andrew thought to say, no, as his father was Mr. McBride, but he realized the title had transferred to his shoulders. "Yes, I am."

"For you, sir." The boy held out the telegram and his palm waited.

"Here." Andrew dropped in a couple of pennies.

"Thank you, sir. Should I stay for a response?"

"No, thank you." Tucking the telegram into his pocket, Andrew picked up the two buckets of milk and aimed for the kitchen. Whatever news had arrived, he didn't want the lad watching him.

His mother took the buckets and began straining the milk through several layers of cheese cloth. "What does it say?"

Andrew opened the yellow envelope and collapsed onto a chair. "God, no. Please, no." He buried his head in his hands and sobbed. Nancy's death was his fault. He should have left her alone. He shouldn't have surprised her but should have written first asking if he might visit.

His mother snatched the paper and leaned against the door jam. "Oh, dear, dear. Suicide. That poor young woman."

"And they say not to come." His hands muffled Andrew's voice. "But she was my wife."

Mrs. McBride dried her hands. "I'll return shortly. I'm going to the McVea's to use their phone."

Andrew wandered from room to room, picking up an embroidered pillow Nancy had made for his parents, gazing at their wedding photo where he held Nancy's hand. He should have listened to Nancy's pleading and installed a phone, but he had explained how they couldn't afford one at that time. And why did they need a phone with the village a short walk away and everyone they knew lived along the lakeshore? The letters from his sisters served them well as the missives could be reread numerous times. But perhaps if he had allowed the phone, Nancy might have stayed. Perhaps if he had agreed to work at a furniture factory in Grand Rapids, she would have lived with him in some small home. But after concocting the lie about Andrew owning a large peach farm, how could Nancy's father explain having a common laborer as a son-in-law.

The screen door swished closed, and his mother led Andrew to the settee. "I connected with Mrs. Phelps. Nancy's father was too indisposed. Last evening, Nancy went for a walk and a policeman spied her standing on the bridge over the Grand River. But before he could reach her, she jumped. With help from some fishermen, the policeman recovered her body."

Andrew groaned. He shouldn't have mentioned the word divorce. He had driven Nancy to suicide and would never forgive himself. His mother gripped his shoulders.

"You mustn't blame yourself. Nancy has struggled for some time. The loss of a child can ruin a woman's health, and the baby blues will take away her will to live."

"But I asked her if she wanted a divorce." Andrew wiped his tears with his palms. "I should have kept my mouth buttoned."

His mother grimaced. "Should haves will not restore her life. Mrs. Phelps repeated that they do not want you at the funeral. It will be a small affair. Why don't you write a condolence note to Nancy's parents? That might ease the distance between our families." Mrs. McBride rose and returned to the kitchen.

Whatever farm work he had planned for the morning could wait. Andrew grabbed his straw hat and ran to the sheep pasture overlooking the Lake. Flopping onto his belly, his hands ripped out clumps of grass as he pressed his face into the earth and sobbed. Although he had lost Nancy a year ago, hope had lingered in his heart or he wouldn't have traveled to see her. Now regrets would torment him, like leaches they would suck away any tidbits of peace. Would he ever feel contentment again? Would grief shadow him for years? Sitting up, he gazed out at the low deep blue waves rippling inland. They slapped a rhythm against the shore as strong as his heartbeat. Closing his eyes, Andrew absorbed the mesmerizing peace of the waves.

Chapter Five

Swinging the milk bucket, Ginny ambled down the road, watching the spring lambs gambol in the McBride's pasture. They leapt and raced around the flock, bleated, and returned to their mothers ready to nurse again. How had she not noticed the joy and innocence of the lambs? Although their summer cook fetched home fresh produce, milk, and eggs from the McBride Farm, Ginny and her parents had traveled past this flock. But her gaze had focused on the Lake and the sky.

Leaning her arms on the pasture fence, Ginny stared out at the shifting blue water and drew inside her the music of the waves and bird song. In Chicago, she only heard the birds who lived in her parent's garden, but here the cries of the gulls and the shriek of a red-tailed hawk pierced the morning. Such sounds rooted her feet to the soil and stitched her to the natural tapestry. When she straightened, Ginny spotted Andrew hunched over wiping his eyes.

What had befallen him? Should she go to Andrew or would her presence interfere and embarrass him? The McBride's screen door slammed, and Ginny turned around. Mrs. McBride dashed through her vegetable garden and across the McVea's pasture, heading home. Mrs. McBride running? Her movements were measured, steady as the arm of pump moving up and down. Something was terribly wrong. Ginny climbed the fence.

Placing a hand on his shoulder, Ginny knelt next to him. "Andrew? What is wrong? Do you feel like talking?"

Andrew lifted his head. Misery filled his red eyes, and tears slicked his cheeks. Green stained his fists, and his hat had tumbled off. Piles of grass littered the ground. Agony etched his face and his confident and purposeful expression had fled.

"Nancy." He shook his head. "Dead."

"Merciful heavens, no. What happened?" Ginny sank onto the grass, her hands quivering.

"Drowned." Andrew pulled out more grass as he released the details.

"I am so, so sorry." Ginny wanted to hold his dirt and grass-stained hand. Even more she wanted to hug him and whisper how this was not his fault. How cruel of Nancy's parents to not allow him to attend the funeral and find a measure of closure. Now, shame would ride on Andrew's back and tether him to Nancy's death.

Andrew straightened and picked up his hat. "You came for milk."

"Yes, but I can wait." Ginny brushed grass off the skirt of her dress and spied Mrs. McBride walking through her garden.

"I'm sorry about the grass. Let me fill your bucket. I need some normalcy." Andrew opened the gate.

"I'll come back later. I forgot, here." Ginny withdrew the lucky stone from her apron pocket and placed it in Andrew's palm. "May it bring you comfort."

She strode toward home. Why had she given the stone to him now? Would he think her crazy? Or would he understand how she wanted him to have a token from the Lake?

***

Raising his hoe, Andrew walloped the yellow dock plant choking the cornstalk. Heat waves rippled between the rows of stalks and sweat poured down his back. Grief knifed his gut as he chopped the dock into tidbits. He had hoped work would numb his thoughts, but the sight of Nancy flying off the bridge looped over and over and over in his mind. How could he erase it? Reaching into his pant pocket, Andrew pulled out his handkerchief and the gray lucky stone tumbled onto the dirt. He picked it up. This one had a star in the center which meant it should bring extra luck. But he felt anything but lucky. Defeated described his world. But Ginny had meant well.

Her tender gaze and sympathetic eyes floated in front of him. In the pasture, he had sought solitude for his grief, but she had recognized his need to express his loss. How had she known? Despite belonging to a wealthy family, Ginny looked beyond herself and into the needs of others. Why? What made her so different?

He mopped his forehead and neck with his handkerchief and resumed hoeing, promising himself a dip in the Lake before supper. Besides his sweat, the cold water could also wash away thoughts of Ginny. When Nancy had skipped his father's funeral, she had shown him how she did not want to be part of his world nor did he belong in hers.

The sun's slanted rays illuminated the orchard as Andrew handed the reins to his mother who stood at the front of the spray wagon. Next to then rose a wooden tower built over a large barrel and topped by a platform. Andrew wished he had another man to hold the spray gun while he pumped the liquid from the barrel. But most fellows either had jobs at the basket factory or tannery and didn't want to work in the evenings.

"Remember to drive slowly. And steady. We want a mist of spray to cover the trees."

"I will. Are you sure you want to do this tonight?"

"Yes, I do. Working helps." Andrew climbed up the sides of the tower as the team stepped forward.

With one arm, he pushed and pulled the pump handle up and down, and in a minute a fine mist dribbled from the spray gun, filling the air with the smell of rotten eggs. Andrew's eyes burned and the sulfur fumes irritated his nose and throat. His peaches needed this spray to prevent them from rotting from a fungus that plagued stone fruit, but he needed more power to shoot the mist deep into the center of the tree. He let go of the pump handle.

"Whoa!" He called and his mother reined in the team.

"We'll both need baths after this," his mother commented as he climbed down.

"Or a dip in the Lake." Andrew wiped his face. "But I need another helper, so I can concentrate on pumping harder."

"The McVea family went to visit her mother this evening." Mrs. McBride retied the strings on her straw hat.

"Hmm. The barrel is full of spray, so we have to use it." Andrew glance down the road. There must be someone around who could lend a hand. Who else might be home? Most of the other farmers were neck deep in their own chores. A halo of coppery blonde hair glowed in the evening sun as Ginny swung her milk bucket. Would she be willing to help?

"What *are* you doing?" Ginny called as she walked into the orchard. "What is that horrible smell?"

"Sulphur. It coats the peaches and prevents them from rotting due to a fungus we call *brown rot*. I built this spray machine over the winter, but we need a third person to run it efficiently."

"But we don't expect you to join us, Miss Madden," Mrs. McBride said. "You know where the milk is stored so fill your bucket."

"I think it would be fun." Ginny set her pail at the edge of the orchard. "I finished all my kitchen chores."

"If you're sure…." Andrew offered Ginny his hand. "You'll end up with some of the spray on you." How could a refined girl like Ginny want to do manual labor?

"Then I'll need to jump in the Lake." Ginny grinned. "But how does this work?"

"I'll pump the spray and you aim the gun into the center of the trees." Andrew wished he had a pair of gloves to protect Ginny's hands. "Here, if you wear my hat, not as much spray will reach your face." Although he longed to see her ankles, he turned his back as Ginny climbed the ladder and onto the platform.

***

Ginny adjusted Andrew's hat so she could still see. The leather band on the inside of it smelled of sweat and something sweet, perhaps and aftershave lotion? On top of the platform, she gazed out at Lake Michigan and over the surrounding landscape dotted with pastures, strawberry patches, and cottages being built. This was better than climbing trees, an activity her mother had prohibited when Ginny reached ten as no young lady of double digits should be seen in such a compromised position. Thank goodness her mother couldn't see her now. Andrew emerged next to her.

"It's a marvelous view," she said.

"Yes, I never grow tired of it." Andrew handed her the spray gun. "Please aim this at the tops of the trees and then into the center so the spray can cover everything."

Ginny gripped the gun with both hands and the wagon began to roll. Besides her, his strong arms raised and lowered the pump handle and the liquid gurgled as it flowed into the hoses connected to her gun. A cloud of spray floated over the trees and she focused the nozzle into the tree's center, and the mist coated the peaches and glossy leaves. When she finished a tree on one side of the platform, Ginny crossed over it and sprayed the tree on the other side. Back and forth she walked as the wagon stopped at each tree. As the sulfur burned her eyes, tears formed, but Ginny let them fall as she concentrated on her job.

So, this was what fruit farmers did. When Ginny had bought peaches, she had never thought about the work to grow her favorite fruit, but only if a particular variety was ripe yet. What else did Andrew have to do? On the other side of the orchard, green strips of grass lay flat on a mowed field. Hadn't he mentioned something about cutting hay? He probably had to chop wood for his mother just as he had secretly split Ginny's logs. When she had stepped to the woodpile to split kindling, she had found a neat stack of both wood and fine sticks ready for her stove. Did the man ever sleep?

"Take a break while my mother turns the team around." Andrew touched her shoulder. "We'll move on to the next row. How are you doing? How are your eyes?"

"They hurt a bit, but they'll be fine." Ginny dabbed at her tears. "How many rows?"

"Because we spray two rows at a time, five more trips." Andrew gripped the pump handle as the wagon stopped by two trees.

The sun had almost set by the time they finished spraying the orchard and headed to the barn. Ginny longed to race to the beach and dive into the waves but had no swimsuit. Her mother would faint when she smelled her daughter. Andrew unhitched and led the team to the barn.

"Come, you can clean up a bit." Mrs. McBride guided Ginny to the wash basin set up outside. "I'll fetch a fresh towel while you wash."

With a bar of brown soap, Ginny lathered her face. Had she ever used anything other than French soaps perfumed with roses or violets? But all she cared about was ridding the sulfur from her skin. Thank goodness her long sleeves had protected her arms. Mrs. McBride handed her a towel.

"Thank you for helping us. Andrew needed to work off his grief." Mrs. McBride pushed back lose strands of hair.

"I understand." Ginny dried her face. Did she, could she understand such grief? She had only experienced the death of her beloved cat, Rosie, and that had occurred years ago. Yet her heart had spoken those words because she wanted to comprehend Andrew's loss.

"What is that stench?" Mrs. Madden called as the screen door closed behind Ginny.

Should she lie and say she had scared a skunk? No, somehow her mother would probably learn the truth. Ginny set the milk bucket in the ice box and noticed the puddle beneath it. Blast it all, she had forgotten to dump the pan that caught the melted drips. She tossed the water out the back door and grabbed her swimming dress from the back of a chair. Stripping off her clothes, she slid into the suit.

"I helped out on the farm for a bit." Ginny called as she raced out the front door and down to the beach. No need to explain what job she had done. Although their shoulders had brushed when she crossed from one side of the tower to the other, Mrs. McBride had chaperoned them so her mother couldn't complain about that aspect of the encounter.

Ginny wished she had brought a bar of soap. But instead, she ran her fingers through her hair while swishing her head back and forth rinsing the spray from her curls. When most of the scent had vanished, Ginny let the waves carry her along the shore. A few other bathers stood in the lake, while others ambled down the beach, but the twilight had shooed most folks inside their cottages or farmhouses. Big George sparkled in the west, at least that was her name for the star that blazed every evening as the sun set. A ribbon of stars emerged as the Milky Way threaded a path across the sky. Her parents called her name. Ginny waded toward the shore, rubbed her towel over her body, and climbed up the dune to where her mother stood.

"It is one thing to cook for your family but doing farm work! Have you lost your mind?"

No, Ginny had found a manner of thinking that appealed to her. "I walked down for milk and saw how the McBride's needed an extra hand. Andrew's mother worked with us, so we were never alone." Ginny stiffened her shoulders; she should have called him Mr. McBride.

"Andrew!" Her mother shook her head. "I think on the next trip for milk your father will escort you. You have spent too much time at that farm. You might as well burn your dress."

"Yes, Mama." Her mother was probably right about the fate of the ruined dress, but Ginny would find a way to convince her father to stay home.

***

Throwing his towel onto the beach, Andrew dove in and out of the waves relishing how they washed away the sulfur and soothed his shattered heart. He had never conceived his marriage would end in suicide. Because of his struggles, Andrew had understood how the death of their child contributed to Nancy's depression. Floating on his back, Andrew stared at the first star of the evening glowing in the west.

Now and then, he would stop at the tiny grave in the Douglas Cemetery and place a bouquet of wildflowers at the granite headstone declaring *Lydia McBride, May 10-May*

11, 1914. Andrew would remember holding his daughter and the dreams of her future he had shared with Nancy. And his mother's concerned expression when Lydia refused to nurse and weaken throughout the night. As the sun rose, Lydia had mewled like a kitten and went limp in Nancy's arms. Nancy's screams had awakened him from his bedside chair. One glance at their baby, and he had comprehended their loss. But instead of welcoming his embrace, Nancy had clutched Lydia and pushed him away.

Tears seeped from Andrew's eyes. That day his marriage had begun to decay, and the rot had spread destroying emotions and dreams until all bonds had crumbled. Now he wasn't even wanted at his wife's funeral. So be it. His mother had warned him about marrying a privileged woman, and he had discovered the truth of her advice. He dragged himself from the Lake and dried off.

But Ginny. Miss Madden defied his mother's classifications. Andrew stared down the shore, sensing Ginny had also rushed into the arms of the waves. With great resolve, the lass had held the spray gun, poking it between branches and releasing the mist. Surely her arms had grown tired, but she hadn't complained even once. His mother's amazed glances had revealed her thoughts about Ginny. Andrew plodded up the dune. Morning would arrive before his body had recovered from today.

Chapter Six

Standing on the back porch, Andrew scratched his freshly shaved chin. The strawberries needed to be picked, and the hay needed to be raked, so this afternoon they could load it onto the wagon. His mother would drive the team, but currently she squatted in her garden harvesting peas to be canned. Why did June in its glory of green leaves and daisies bring so much work all demanding to be completed at the same time? Grabbing a few tin pails, Andrew strode to the strawberry patch and knelt.

The four-hundred-foot-long rows hadn't felt so lengthy when he and his mother had planted the strawberry patch. But by the time he reached the end of the first of the four rows, Andrew questioned why had he decided to grow strawberries? Yesterday, the pale red berries had glowed among the leaves, but raccoon paw prints in the sandy soil explained why so few berries remained. Overnight, the critters had eaten the ripe berries, leaving behind pink and pale green fruit. Come evening, he would have to sit with his gun and blast the furry beasts or he would have no berries to sell. Slipping his fingers beneath a crown of leaves, he plucked a large hidden red berry, and popped it into his mouth. For a flick of a butterfly's wing, he wished he could have slid that berry between Ginny's lips.

After finishing the second row, Andrew deposited the buckets of berries in a patch of shade on the back porch. He harnessed his horses and hooked up the hay rake to his team. Sitting on the metal seat, Andrew slapped the reins, and his horses stepped towards the hay field where he lowered the rake so the long, curved iron spikes would comb the mowed grass and pile it into strips. Andrew clicked his tongue, the team leaned into their harness and the rake whirred. Other than calling out commands and raising the rake as the horses turned right, Andrew allowed his mind to rest and dwell in the moment.

The jingle of the harness and the song of the meadowlark floated across the land as a rabbit darted from one ribbon of hay to another. When the team turned, a glimpse of low waves rolling towards shore promised Andrew another evening swim. Or perhaps even a quick dip before the noon meal. Wasn't he a lucky fellow to live where others came for a respite from cities? For the thousandth time, he wondered why Nancy had liked visiting the lakeshore for a summer holiday but had complained about living here. Andrew couldn't imagine residing anywhere but here. When he finished raking the hay, he unhitched his team and rubbed them down.

"Someone needs to take those strawberries to the Butler," his mother said as he stepped into the kitchen. "It's too warm to let them sit outside for long. Maybe they would purchase some of these peas, as I won't have time to pod all of them before we load hay. And we need the cash as the debt for the sheep pasture is due in the fall."

"I guess I'll go." Andrew slid into his chair and said grace. One more job to squeeze into the day. He hated how each week his mother brought up the topic of the looming debt. The peach crop should pay back the loan and provide plenty of income for other expenses.

***

Ginny recognized Andrew's team by the white heart on the forehead of one horse as they stood by the back door of the Butler Hotel. What had brought him to town this morning? A screen door opened, Andrew emerged and lifted a half-bushel basket filled with something green.

"Papa, let's go say hello to Andrew." Ginny placed her hand on her father's arm.

"Don't let your mother hear you call him by his first name. I should order him to never ask you to work on that spraying contraption."

Ginny frowned. "Papa! I doubt if I will."

This morning, her skin still tingled from the irritating spray and her eyes remained a faint pink. She had worn a large hat with a veil to conceal her face and to appease her mother. The trip to town to seek a source for the crown roast had been her mother's idea, but Ginny and her father had not discovered anyone who could help them. Crossing the dirt road, they walked to the back of the Butler Hotel as Andrew exited.

"Good morning," Ginny said. "It's good to see you taking a break from farming."

"Good morning, Mr. Madden, Miss Madden." Andrew nodded. "I had to deliver some strawberries and peas for the Butler. I should be home greasing our hay loader which is the next job to tackle."

"Make hay while the sun shines and all that?" Mr. Madden said.

"Yes, sir. What brings you to town?" Andrew removed his hat and wiped his forehead with his handkerchief.

"A crown roast for a dinner party. My wife is determined to serve one," Mr. Madden said. "But we haven't found anyone butchering a pig."

"No, most folks slaughter their hogs in the fall when it's cooler. But I might know someone who can help you. Come with me, sir." Andrew opened the door to the kitchen. "Charlie!"

A tall man with gray hair wearing a spattered white apron covering his white shirt and black pants emerged from behind a hot stove. "I thought you had brought everything in."

"This is Charlie Campbell, the main cook for the Butler. Please meet Mr. Madden and his daughter, Miss Madden. They need a crown roast."

"When do you want it?" Charlie scratched the back of his neck.

"In two weeks, please, sir," Ginny said. "Can you help us?"

"Hopefully. A farmer over by Fennville is supposed to butcher a hog for us and I could tell him to cut a roast instead of pork chops. He's dropping off a load of chickens tomorrow, so I can ask him then."

"Thank you, sir." Mr. Madden began to pull out a billfold.

"Thank you, but please wait to pay when I know more." Charlie mopped his forehead. "I need to get cracking."

"Me, too. It's just mother and me loading hay this afternoon." Andrew tipped his hat. "Would you two like a ride home?"

"Yes, please," Ginny said.

Her father gave his hand to her as Ginny climbed onto the wagon seat and he circled to the other side. Sitting next to Andrew, Ginny adjusted her hat so it wouldn't touch his shoulders, but as his thighs brushed hers, a flash of heat swirled through her. Sometimes when a dancing partner had slipped his hand onto her waist, her flesh had shivered, but Andrew's touch sent a lightning bolt. Her mother had hoped to keep her from Andrew, but instead, new feelings bubbled inside Ginny.

"Comfortable?" Andrew asked. "Hopefully, the ferry is on the Saugatuck side, so we won't have to wait."

"I'll pay the fee. It sounds as if you have a lot to do," Mr. Madden said.

"Thank you, sir. There's always more work than I can manage by myself or with my mother. After the hay, I need to finish picking strawberries."

"I could do that." Ginny glanced at her father. "I wouldn't be holding a spray gun."

"I am sorry if you disapproved, sir, but I am grateful that Ginny helped us. We dearly needed a third person." Andrew drew on the reins, and they stopped at the ferry landing.

"I understand, but she is not to help in that manner, again." Mr. Madden hopped down, paid the fee, and Andrew drove the wagon onto the flat vessel.

"But what about picking strawberries, Papa? That's not so different from picking flowers, and Mama does that." Ginny climbed off the wagon and leaned on the ferry's railing. Two other riders sat on a bench.

"I have to admit, sir, it would be a blessing if Ginny could harvest those two rows."

Mr. Madden exhaled. "Very well. In gratitude for finding a crown roast, Ginny may pick berries."

After adjusting her wide-brim straw hat, Ginny knelt by the row of strawberries. A flock of crows cawed as they circled the peach orchard and nearby a kill-deer's cry sliced the silence. As Ginny reached into a plant, a thin brown snake slithered away, and she squealed. She hadn't thought how snakes and spiders might lurk in the plants. The sun and mosquitoes had appeared the biggest threats to her comfort, but long sleeves and her hat should prevent sunburn and bites.

Ginny picked a handful of berries, dropped them into a tin bucket and nibbled on a plump warm strawberry. Its juice oozed through her lips as intense flavor coated her tongue. Images of whipped cream heaped onto strawberry shortcake or strawberry ice cream filled her mind. Somewhere in the pantry she had spotted the faded green bucket of their White Mountain Ice Cream Freezer. Maybe she could wheedle a quart of cream from Mrs. McBride.

***

As his mother called to the team, Andrew plunged his pitchfork into the hay tumbling onto the wagon and tossed it to the front. The scent of warm, dry grass and his sweat mingled as he repeated the motions over and over and the mound of hay expanded. The rattling of chains driving the machine and the clanking of the long metal arms as their claws scooped the hay onto the moving conveyor belt numbed his hearing. Andrew sneezed but kept on loading the hay until the pile reached his feet.

"Whoa!" He called and his mother reined in the team. Andrew disengaged the hay loader, it shuddered to a stop, and he climbed back onto the wagon. "To the barn."

Sitting on top of the hay, Andrew gazed at Ginny working her way down a row, eating a few berries, and plopping more in the bucket. She paused and wiped her face with her hanky, glanced up at him and waved. On the next trip, Andrew would invite her to ride on the load as Ginny probably had never experienced such a moment. Would she be frightened, or would her curiosity propel her to climb up and perch beside him?

When they reached the barn, Andrew positioned the wagon beneath a large iron claw with jaws that opened as he pulled on attached ropes. The teeth dug into the hay, he closed the jaws, and a different rope dragged the contraption along a metal track until it reached an empty spot in the loft. With the first rope, Andrew released the jaws and the hay tumbled out. The sight of the stored hay filled him with satisfaction and the security that his animals would eat well in the winter. When he had emptied the wagon, his mother handed him a mug of cold water.

"How are you holding up?" She sipped from her mug.

"All right. It would be easier with another worker, but here we are." Andrew dribble some of the water down his neck so it could wash away the coating of green leaves.

Thank goodness he could look forward to swimming in Lake Michigan.

"Yes, this would go quicker if your father was alive." Mrs. McBride soaked her hanky and washed her face. "It's nice that Miss Madden offered to pick. One less job for this evening."

"Yes." Andrew downed another mug of water. "We better keep going."

As the wagon rolled back to the field, Andrew hoped Ginny's parents wouldn't view picking strawberries as beneath their daughter's station, because then she might be allowed to help again. Her father appeared like a reasonable fellow, but from listening to Ginny's mother on the wagon ride to their cottage, Mrs. Madden sounded like Nancy's mother. He had endured enough from those sorts of women.

Andrew pitched the final bits of hay onto the green pile and stopped the hay loader. Jumping down, he walked over to Ginny who picked the last couple of plants. Pink tinted her fingers and her mouth.

"Would you like a hayride?" He nodded towards the wagon. "It's the last load."

"What about these berries? I put the rest of the buckets in the shade like you asked." Ginny stood and stretched her back.

"We won't be gone long. Please come." Andrew smiled at the streaks of pink strawberry juice on Ginny's cheek where she had slapped a bug. His lips yearned to kiss the pink juice and find their way to her mouth.

***

Holding Andrew's hand, Ginny set one foot onto the hay wagon and Andrew pulled her up. His rough fingers scratched her skin, yet she tingled at the feel of his strength. How could she scale the slippery slope of dried grass?

"Let me climb a head of you and then I can help you to the top."

Andrew's muscular thighs stretched his trousers and Ginny blushed. Her mother would swoon if she witnessed this scene. Offering his hand, Andrew drew her to half-way up the pile before he scrambled to the top. Leaning over, he slipped his hands beneath her arm pits and lifted to the summit. Although the sun had warmed her, a different heat quivered in her belly and raced over her flesh. No man had touched her in that manner.

"I'm sorry. That was a bit forward," Andrew said.

Ginny exhaled. "That's all right. I doubt if I could have climbed up without your assistance."

She couldn't think of another man whom she wanted to hold her and wished his hands had found her waist. Mrs. McBride clucked to the horses and the wagon moved. Ginny ducked when they rolled beneath overhanging branches. The mound swayed as one wagon wheel dipped into a rut and Ginny clutched Andrew's arm. Looking out over the orderly rows of peach trees and strawberry plants revealed the size of Andrew's farm. No wonder he spoke of needing more workers or more hours in a day. Yet from helping, she comprehended the satisfaction in accomplishing a task. Somehow, she would convince her father to allow her to continue with the strawberry harvest.

***

Andrew dipped his spoon into a bowl filled with crumbled cornbread, milk and two poached eggs. How could his mother drive the team, walk into the kitchen, and cook a fast supper while he milked? Her years of farming living had prepared her for the task, but even when he and his sisters were children, she had managed. Nancy had complained about cooking for two people. While a part of him ached over her death, he *had* been single for over a year. Now and then Nancy's presence darted into his mind, but mostly he thought about what he needed to accomplish on the farm. Or he paused to admire the beauty of the waves on Lake Michigan.

His mother pushed a plate of radishes in his direction. "I unpacked your black armbands from the trunk in the attic. Do you think I should rehang the mourning wreath on our door?"

Andrew swallowed a bite of radish. "No. Do you really think the bands are necessary?"

"People will wonder." His mother sipped from her glass of water.

"How many people will know of her death? Her family won't say much because it was a suicide." Out of their shame, the Phelps would hide the details and pay the newspapers to not print the story of Nancy's death.

From what he could remember Nancy had made no friends with the villagers. Only family members had attended the funeral for their baby. When his father had died, he and his mother had needed to display their grieving hearts by wearing black. But over the past year they had dealt with Nancy's empty chair at the table.

"I told our minister and of course the McVea family." His mother sprinkled salt on her eggs.

"And Miss Madden knows." Andrew bit into another radish.

"Yes." His mother stared at him. "Be careful Andrew."

"As you have seen, she's not like Nancy. And at the end of the summer, her family will return to Chicago."

"Thank goodness."

"I'm off for a swim." Andrew shoved in his chair and carried his dishes to the sink.

Rising from the waves, Andrew combed his fingers through his hair and tucked it behind his ears. In his blue and navy striped swimsuit, the short sleeves exposed his arms, and the legs of the suit reached his knees. While Andrew enjoyed how the outfit allowed him freedom when swimming, his mother questioned the appropriateness of walking the beach while half-naked. After rubbing himself with a towel, he draped it across his shoulders and walked south toward Ginny's cottage.

He spotted her wearing the blue sailor dress and short bloomers, floating on her back, her hair a copper cloud. Her shapely calves dangled below the water, but her slim arms stretched outward. What would it feel like if she wrapped those arms around his neck? Andrew blushed at how such thoughts bubbled up and the heat they produced that simmered in his veins.

"Hallo," he called. "The Lake feels wonderful after working hard."

Ginny popped up. Her wet suit clung to her bosom and the bloomers had inched up, exposing her knees. He should look away, but Andrew couldn't turn from memorizing her curves. Yearning to kiss her flooded him.

"Oh, good evening." Ginny waded in. "Perfect for a stroll."

Instead of picking up her towel, Ginny's bare feet stepped closer. Andrew swallowed. How he would like to run his lips along her fine collar bone, inhaling her sweetness and the softness of her skin. After experiencing married nights with Nancy, he had been single too long.

"Yes, out for a stroll. To see the sunset. Would you like to join me?"

***

Ginny glanced around. Only a few strangers staying at one of the cottages in Shorewood sat on a quilt. Her parents had gone to visit the Mitchell family this evening and wouldn't be home until dark. She would return before them.

"Yes, I'd like that." Ginny reached for her towel, aware of Andrew's eyes absorbing her figure. While drying her hair through half-closed eyes she admired his muscular calves and the swell of his biceps expanding the short sleeves. To hug Andrew would be like when she had stretched her arms around the rough bark of a huge burr oak tree. Solid and firm, tall and mighty.

"Which direction?" Andrew asked. "There's fewer people down my way."

Ginny wished he could offer his elbow, but because of their bare arms, they could not participate in that politeness. Instead, she walked as close to Andrew as she dared breathing in his manly scent while watching the sand for lucky stones.

"Look!" She scooped up the gray disk. "You bring good luck. Since meeting you, I've found six lucky stones."

"What do you do with them?"

"I'm stringing them into a garland and when it's long enough, I'll decorate my room with it." Ginny tucked the lucky stone into a small pocket located over her heart.

"You'll need hundreds of them." Andrew squatted down and pushed aside some gravel.

"I know, but I'll have dozens of summers to find them. If you see any, please collect them for me." Ginny brushed her big toe against Andrew's.

"I will. Usually, I spy them after storms." Andrew stood up. "Look at the sun."

"Incredible. Look at the waves, like liquid amber." Ginny yearned for Andrew to take her hand. Shifting her weight, her fingers touched his and slid away. He glanced down at her.

"The same color as your beautiful hair. You shine with the fire of the sunset." Andrew twined his fingers with her as the sun dipped into the lake.

Ginny cherished his callouses, his rough fingernails, and his thick knuckles. Other men had taken her hand, but none had held it with a strength honed through hard labor on the land he loved.

Chapter Seven

Picking up a pencil, Ginny began to write as her mother dropped items into a large canvas duffle bag and dictated.

"Six linen napkins, one tablecloth, two sets of cotton sheets, two petticoats, six drawers, five men's undershirts." Mrs. Madden stuffed those deeper into the bag.

"Is this really necessary, Mother? Has the laundress ever stolen from us?"

"No, but once my drawers were sent to the Morris family and they recognized my initial on the waistband. Would you like their son to see your undergarments?"

"No." Ginny cringed. Samuel Morris would love to unbutton her drawers while she wore them, but she didn't want to even take his elbow when offered. Now if Andrew should lift her skirt, she would be tempted to slide them off.

"By the way, I invited the Morris family to the dinner party and Samuel will accompany them."

"Please don't sit him near me." At the gathering at his home, Mrs. Morris had placed Samuel's seat next to Ginny. Beneath the table, she had swatted away his hand when he had attempted to fondle her thigh. Thank goodness for petticoats and a linen skirt sheltering her limbs.

"And why not? His family owns one of the largest meat packing facilities in Chicago."

"I suppose I'll be busy serving everyone, so I guess it doesn't matter." Ginny brushed eraser crumbs off her list. She hoped to avoid the annoying and pointless conversations that circled at dinner parties. What would they think if she described what if felt like to ride on a load of hay?

"While you will prepare the meal, Mrs. Sandford will lend me her maid who will serve us."

"I assume Mr. and Mrs. Sandford are coming, too?" But hopefully not their rakish son, though it might be fun to see James and Samuel compete for her attentions.

"Of course, James will dine with us." Mrs. Madden sat up straighter. "Remember, this party is for your benefit so these eligible young men can view your charms and refinements. So, behave."

"Yes, Mother." Ginny glanced at the clock on the mantel. "We had better finish the list. They pick up in twenty minutes."

"Six white dresses. Six pairs of white hose. Five men's shirts." Mrs. Madden slipped the garments into the bag.

***

Andrew kicked at the yellow peach leaves littering the dirt. What was happening? His father had told stories about two diseases that had ravaged the lakeshore in the 1880's. The first one named "the peach yellows" turned the leaves faint gold and the peaches ripened a good week earlier. A red line had streaked the peach's flesh from the pit to the skin. But his peaches didn't look as if they had ripened early. The second disease called "the little peach" caused the green fruit to wither. His father had described how the only solution was to chop down the orchards and burn the trees. If a farmer had refused to destroy his trees, the county sent in a commission to rip out the orchard and charged the poor fellow a fee. Andrew wished his father were here to figure out this problem.

At the end of the branches, clusters of leaves drooped. As he broke off the twig, several mottled brown and gray moths fluttered away and landed in a nearby tree. He had never seen this insect in his orchard. Had it caused the damage to the ends of the twigs and the dying leaves? Cupping his hands, Andrew snapped them around a moth and crushed the insect's head. He would send it to the Agricultural College in East Lansing and see what they knew about this pest.

***

Leaning back in her rocker, Ginny stared at the bushel of pea pods. One hour of work had lowered the basket by two inches. How could she finish this task among the many dinner party chores looming before her? Mrs. Sandford's maid could set the table as she would know how to arrange the silverware and the proper placing of water goblets and wine glasses. Ginny rubbed her sore wrists, slit a pea pod with a fingernail, and rolled six plump peas into a bowl sitting in her lap. After delivering the peas, she wished

Andrew could have stayed and helped her, but the brief experiences on his farm had shown her the numerous chores he and his mother had to manage. Footsteps sounded on the kitchen floor, and her father cleared his throat. Ginny's shoulder's stiffened as she waited for a lecture.

"Would you like some help?" Her father pulled up a chair. "You'll have to show me what to do."

"Here" Ginny handed him an empty bowl. "I drop the pods in that basket and the shelled peas in the bowl.

Her father's fingers fumbled with the pod as he snapped it open and pushed out the peas. They pinged into the bowl until enough covered the bottom and muffled the sound. Ginny waited for him to remark about how her choices had made her a slave to the kitchen, but he concentrated on the job. Outside a wren trilled from a honeysuckle bush, and Lake Michigan's low waves whispered along the shore. After fifteen minutes, Ginny relaxed, appreciating how the level of pods was diminishing. More footsteps and her mother's perfume floated onto the porch.

"Mr. Madden! What are you doing?" Her mother's voice rose. "If you had found a decent cook, your daughter's fingers wouldn't be turning green."

"True, but it's nice to spend time with Ginny, listening to the birds and sharing a job. Remember how my parents went into service when they arrived from Ireland." Mr. Madden dropped a handful of peas into his bowl. "Plus, I'm tired of reading about the war over in Europe and women marching for the right to vote."

"Well, I never." Mrs. Madden's skirts swooshed as she fled back into the dining room.

"Thank you, Papa." Ginny gazed at her father. Little lines fanned out by his blue eyes, but his forehead was smooth, and a ruddy tint colored his cheeks. He needed this holiday at the cottage as much as she did.

"You're welcome. While I've agreed to this experiment, I still expect you to make a good match. You don't have to marry either of the lads coming tonight, but you will wed from Chicago's society."

"Yes, Papa." Like a cat's claws raked against a tree, his words scratched at the memories of Andrew's strong fingers linked with hers. If Ginny didn't want to unite her future with a meat packing baron or wealthy lawyer, she would need to find a way to remain in Douglas.

When they had finished with the peas, Mr. Madden stretched his arms over his head with his hands clasped together. "While that felt good, I wouldn't want to do it again any time soon. Looks like you forgot to dump the ice box pan." He nodded to where a puddle had spread beneath the ice box and beyond.

"Oh, no! Ice!" Ginny had forgotten to order extra ice to keep her dinner party's supplies cold. Running to the puddle, she pulled out the tin pan and poured the water into the sink. She didn't have time to go to town nor could she carry home a four-pound block of ice, plus she needed to start the roast. Her father's hand rested on her shoulder as she blinked back tears. How was she going to keep the cream cold enough so it would whip into a fluffy mound?

"This is why I should have hired a cook. Coordinating everything for a dinner party is too demanding for you. If I had a buggy, I would go fetch ice."

"Perhaps Andrew or his mother are going into Douglas. Could you go see if they could bring me some ice?" Ginny wiped her eyes.

***

Andrew stuffed three moths into the envelope holding his letter and sealed it. With such warm temperatures, he should mail his message today so the insects wouldn't rot before reaching East Lansing. In the kitchen, his mother added a rubber ring to a jar, screwed on a zinc lid and placed the blue jar in a canning kettle filled with steaming water. She wouldn't be able to leave the kitchen for several hours, so he had better go to Douglas. He might as well hitch the team and pick up the sacks of flour and salt his mother needed.

Andrew slapped the reins and the team walked down the road. Heat waves rose from the sand, and a cicada buzzed from an overarching tree branch. Outside a cottage, three girls in short-sleeved calico frocks played tag. Squinting, Andrew spied Mr. Madden marching toward him. Was something wrong at their cottage? Or was her father headed to his farm to lecture him about Ginny working? When they met, Andrew pulled on the reins.

"I was coming to see you," Mr. Madden said. "Ginny forgot to buy more ice. If you are going into Douglas, may I ride along?"

"Certainly. Climb up." Andrew clutched the reins. Would Mr. Madden appreciate his offer of transportation, or would sitting next to him bring criticism about Ginny riding on the load of hay?

Silence drifted between the men with the only sounds the creaking of the harness and the thud of horses' hooves. Andrew knew Ginny's mother disapproved of him, but her father *had* agreed to his daughter picking strawberries, though only for that one time. Had Mr. Madden discovered how Ginny and held his hand? Andrew shifted his weight. If a lecture was coming, then he wished Mr. Madden would speak.

"Thank you for the ride. I'm afraid preparing for this dinner party has frayed Ginny's nerves. It's too much for my girl. Surely, you know of a woman who could cook for us?"

"No, I'm sorry, but I don't." Andrew shook his head. Like any good father, Mr. Madden wanted to help his daughter, but Ginny had told Andrew how she enjoyed cooking. Yet with the dog days of summer creeping closer, she might want some relief from a hot wood cookstove. He would ask his mother for some quick recipes that didn't need to be baked in an oven.

"I'm sorry about the loss of your late wife," Mr. Madden said. "I'm sure you were shocked."

"Yes, none of us expected it." Andrew drew on the right rein and the team turned onto Ferry Street. He needed to steer the conversation away from himself. "Have you been having a pleasant holiday?"

"Yes, though I may need to take a quick trip to Chicago to see to some business. The missus wants to come along, but I don't want to leave Ginny by herself. I don't think that's a good idea, do you?" Mr. Madden steel blue eyes met Andrew's.

"No, I suppose it isn't." Andrew tugged on the reins and they stopped outside the general store. "Why don't you have them load the ice while I mail this letter."

Andrew jumped down and pushed open the door. Did Mr. Madden have to be so outspoken about his daughter?

Hadn't he shown Ginny respect? Of course, his thoughts wandered to her lips and slender neck and her molten cloud of hair as she floated in the Lake. He probably wasn't the only fellow whose gaze lingered on Ginny's calves when she waded from the water. The girl had slipped her hand into his. While he could have brushed her fingers away, they had twined together as a perfect fit.

"Thanks." Andrew paid the postal clerk for a sheet of stamps, licked two and stuck them on his envelope. Hopefully within a week, he would learn what insect had invaded his farm.

***

As sweat cascaded down her back, Ginny kneaded the wad of bread dough until it turned soft and pliable. Perspiration soaked the back of her dress bodice and formed circles by her armpits. She would have no time for a dip in Lake Michigan this afternoon. At the academy for young females, Mrs. Thorne had taught how ladies were supposed to *glow* but never appear sweaty. But Mrs. Thorne had never cooked on a wood stove in late June. Ginny divided the dough, shaped twelve dinner rolls, and set them in a pan to rise.

After adding another chunk of wood to the fire, Ginny peeked into the oven where the crown roast glistened as grease ran down its sides. The sweet fragrance of pork and sage filled the kitchen, as Ginny scrubbed the new potatoes and set them into a kettle. Bootsteps sounded on the porch and her father opened the screen door. Andrew carried a large block of ice.

"Please place it inside the ice box," Mr. Madden said.

"Thank you!" Ginny ran and opened the metal door.

"You're welcome." Andrew shoved the block inside the tin cubicle and wiped his hands on his pants. "Everything ready for tonight? Smells wonderful."

"I think so. Please thank your mother for the tips for roasting pork." Ginny smiled up at Andrew.

"Thank you for the ride," Mr. Madden said and walked into the dining room.

"Have a pleasant evening." Andrew chucked Ginny under the chin.

His fingerprints tingled and Ginny wanted to run after Andrew. What did that endearment mean? Was Andrew flirting with her or did he have serious affections? She wished she could serve this meal to him and not to the people invited.

When Mrs. Sandford's maid arrived, Ginny gave her the linen tablecloth and napkins and showed her the shelf holding their best china and the silverware chest. Ginny ran into her room, sponged off the sweat slicking her back and breasts, changed into a fresh frock and pinned her hair. Her mother would not approve of her simple white dress, but she still had cooking to finish. Thankfully, her mother had snipped and folded sheets of paper to form the little white crowns to adorn the roast. Tying on a clean apron, Ginny marched into her kitchen.

Her hard work had transformed the room in *her* kitchen where light brown bread rolls cooled, and peas and new potatoes simmered. A golden sponge cake filled a tin pan, and in the ice box sat a bowl of sliced strawberries. Ginny would whip the cream just before serving the shortcake. Tomorrow, she would thank Andrew's mother for recipes and advice.

Someone knocked on the cottage's front door and her mother welcomed their guests. Ginny glanced at the kitchen screen door, where Andrew's hands had rested on it. Being proper gentlemen, Samuel Morris and James Sandford wouldn't touch the kitchen screen door, and it would remain Andrew's portal into her world and her heart.

Did she genuinely love him or was Andrew a novelty to experience like a boat ride down the Kalamazoo River? While Ginny ladled peas and potatoes into a serving bowl, images of Andrew standing in his wet striped swimsuit floated through her memory. Square shoulders, firm biceps, muscular thighs, and calves thatched with dark brown hair. When she had brushed her toes against his, an ache had flowed through her. Kissing Andrew would be like eating his ripe strawberries filled with sweet perfume and a sweetness that had lingered on her tongue.

"Your mother says I should take over so you can chat with your guests, Miss Madden." Mrs. Sanford's maid stood in the doorway.

"Any last questions?" Ginny removed her apron and patted her hair.

"No, you gave good instructions, Miss. You've worked hard." The maid's eyes traveled over the steaming roast pork adorned with the crowns.

"Thank you." Ginny hoped her mother would feel the same emotions. Lifting her chin, she walked into the dining room and looked out at the Lake. No matter what happened tonight, from her seat she would keep her focus on the waves and their music. No foolish young gentleman could rob her of inner peace.

Knives and forks tapped against the china plates as everyone enjoyed the meal. The maid circled the table, offering another serving of the pork or vegetables. Ginny glanced at the guests' expressions of pleasure. How rewarding to create a dinner and know that others appreciated it. Her mother's face wore the necessary smile of a hostess as she led the conversation down respectable paths such as a new show at the Chicago Institute of Arts or the up-coming opera season. Ginny loved those events, too, but why not discuss the beauty of the dunes, the feel of the wind in her cheeks or the field of daisies blooming near Andrew's farm.

James Sandford shoved back his chair and raised his wine glass. "I propose a toast to Miss Madden, whose hidden cooking skills astound me."

Samuel Morris jumped to his feet. "To Miss Madden! A wonderful woman who would make a gracious homemaker!"

Their parents remained seated, but they lifted their glasses and nodded at her. Ginny murmured her thanks and stared at her napkin. Her mother's rosy cheeks portrayed her anger. Would her mother abandon her views about cooking and accept Ginny's passion for homemaking? No, probably not, but at least for tonight Ginny could bask in the praises. Yet a squiggle of apprehension ran down her spine, were these two fellows competing for her hand?

"Oh, my goodness. Look at that glorious sunset." Mrs. Madden stood up. "Why don't we go outside and watch it while the maid clears these dishes. Then we can return for dessert."

Although Ginny wanted to avoid both James and Samuel, they rushed to the front porch door and James held it open. Samuel nodded at him and offered his arm to Ginny. She shook her head and brushed by them, skipping down the steps and marching to the lip of the dune. While she would relish slipping her elbow with Andrew's arm, she wasn't a delicate seashell needing coddling. Hadn't these two hypocrites praised her as an amazing woman? As Ginny joined the small flock, the look on her mother's face showed she had witnessed the scene and would rebuke Ginny tomorrow. But for now, the success of the dinner party still rested on Ginny dishing up a wonderful dessert.

***

Barefoot with his sleeves rolled up and his shirt halfway unbutton, Andrew strolled north on the beach toward Ginny's cottage. He shouldn't spy, but he hoped for a glimpse of Ginny, an image to float before his eyes when he fell asleep tonight instead of visions of yellow peach leaves. Laughter rippled from outside the Madden cottage. Andrew squatted down and hid by a thicket of waving dune grass.

Dressed in linen suits and straw boaters the two young men hovered like yellow jackets next to Ginny who stared at the sunset. While they chattered, she merely nodded her head. The older couples strolled back to the cottage and took chairs on the front porch. What were those fellows saying to Ginny? Andrew assumed these preapproved men were candidates for marriage while others lingered back in Chicago. He considered joining the little party, but he hadn't been invited and knew Ginny's parents wouldn't welcome him.

Nancy's red eyes and pale face flickered through Andrew's mind and he sighed. How much had he and the farm contributed to her death? If she had married within her social class, would Nancy still live? Ginny might enjoy picking strawberries or riding on a load of hay or even her current homemaking activities, but after a year or two would she still find pleasure in them? If Andrew sincerely loved her, wouldn't it be kinder to stamp out any growing affections and encourage Ginny to accept her position? While his heart would ache, he wanted what was best for her. His mother and her parents would applaud such a decision. Andrew turned and walked home.

***

Ginny wanted to shove James and Samuel off the edge of the dune and into the Lake. All they could talk about was themselves: how their businesses were thriving, how James had built a tennis court on their property while Samuel had jumped his horse over a wide creek. Did they think these things mattered to her? To speak of how much money they had earned would have displayed a vulgar behavior, but to extoll their recent purchases showed off their wealth. The louts couldn't fork on a wagon load of hay. Ginny yawned and patted her mouth.

"Dessert, gentlemen?" She picked up her skirt and strode to the cottage. If not for the maid, she could duck out early and wash the dishes. One more hour and politeness would send the guests home.

Chapter Eight

Under a bruised sky, thunder rolled across the Lake and rattled the windowpanes. Ginny dashed about the cottage slamming windows closed while watching the squall line race closer. A lone sailing vessel sped towards the mouth of the Kalamazoo River. Lightening etched the horizon in numerous locations as the storm sent the first showers. Ginny stood on the front porch, relishing the mist floating through the screens and cooling her flesh. Had her parents decided to wait out the storm at the Sandford cottage? Like a shawl dragged across the Lake, the rain textured the water as the wind bent the dune grass and oak saplings. Thunder roared as the lightning struck something to the south.

Darkness like thick wool surrounded the cottage. A blast of wind pushed Ginny inside and she collapsed onto a chair as rain cascaded against the window. Pea-size hail pinged against the glass and drummed on the cottage roof. Ginny liked storms, but this one was a whirlwind of black, gray waterfalls, and molten lightning. The gale shook the cottage like a cat playing with a rat. Noticing water sluicing over the sun porch windowsills, Ginny grabbed towels and pressed them against the current. Curling up on the chair seat, she counted the seconds between lightning and thunderclaps willing the gale to move inland.

What was Andrew doing during this storm? Was he standing in his barn comforting his animals or drinking coffee in the kitchen with his mother while nibbling molasses cookies? Although Ginny had learned only a little about farm life, she sensed how adverse weather could affect Andrew's crops. She hugged her knees to her chest and prayed protection for his harvest.

After a supper of cold roast pork, reheated peas and potatoes plus the dinner rolls, Mr. Madden set his knife and fork at the upper right arc of his dinner plate. Ginny swallowed her last bite of roll as her father sipped his wine. From the gloating look on her mother's face, she was thrilled about something.

"Ginny, thank you for preparing a wonderful feast yesterday, but your mother and I have made a decision."

Here it comes. A snare to remove her from her kitchen and drag her into society. Ginny balled her fists in her lap. Why couldn't her parents give her one summer to revel in cooking?

"Mrs. Sandford connected us with a fellow attending the Saugatuck Summer School of Painting. For his tuition and housing payment, he works in the boarding house's kitchen during breakfast and lunch. Starting tomorrow, Mr. Francis Chapin will cook our dinners, wash the dishes, and tidy up the kitchen."

"This will provide free afternoons to visit with our friends instead of hiding in the kitchen. Mrs. Sandford asked us to share tea tomorrow." Mrs. Madden folded her napkin and placed it by her plate.

"I was going to search for lucky stones." If Ginny had to share her kitchen with a man, then she would find comfort walking the beach, preferably toward the south.

Her father frowned. "I think it is time for you to cease with childish games. You need to focus on more womanly pursuits."

"If you would prefer an older suiter, William is here for the rest of the summer. He hopes in two years to run as a representative for the United States Congress. Obviously, he needs a wife to attend functions with him and perhaps even give him a baby." Mrs. Madden gazed at Ginny. "I'm eager to become a grandmother."

"People expect their elected officials to have families," Mr. Madden said.

"I thought William was engaged to Miss Brandenburg?" Ginny shuddered.

"William ended the engagement when he discovered how Miss Brandenburg had taken liberties with the family butler. But you needn't worry about William treating you in that manner," her father said. "He is a respectable gentleman."

Ginny pressed her palms against her thighs and squeezed her lips into a tight line. It was useless to give her opinion about William's lust for gambling. Her father would point out how buying and selling stocks meant taking a risk with his money.

"After his family, I own the next largest share of stock in their company. A merger between our families would enhance William's fortune and ensure me a place on their board. A position I have longed for since you were born." Her father shoved back his chair. "It is time for you to consider your responsibilities to your family and your future."

"His mother told me how he admires you," her mother added. "I think you should wear your pink lawn with a blue sash to highlight your eyes and blushing cheeks."

Ginny didn't want to help some man increase his stockholdings or make babies so he could run for Congress. While she hoped her father might gain the coveted board position, he could earn it without sacrificing her happiness. There was only one man who sparked a longing for marriage. She would rather spray peach trees than serve tiny sandwiches and bite back her words so as not to incite the gossips. Or pick strawberries under the June sun instead of suffering through the mindless meetings of the Women's Club. She needed to discover a way to escape from returning to Chicago and the web of society.

***

Despite a constant drizzle, Andrew moved a fallen limb from the aisle between the rows of peach trees. Green peaches littered the earth beneath each tree along with snapped off clusters of leaves and twigs. One tree had split in half while others had shed branches. Like it or not, he had to carve out the time to clean up this mess. He might as well hitch the team to the wagon and begin hauling away the debris. While he could tidy the orchard, Andrew couldn't glue back the fallen fruit and restore his harvest. He bent down a branch inspecting for hail damage. A few dings, but the peaches might not reveal the bruises until they ripened.

Staring at his wet boots, Andrew rubbed his palms over his cheeks. He had hoped for a good harvest to pay off the debt for the sheep pasture, but he would barely earn enough to cover the costs of spray, baskets, and other expenses. And what might he need to purchase to battle those odd moths? He pushed the vision of Ginny holding a spray gun from his mind. The storm had erased any chance of income that could support a wife.

Andrew hitched the team to a small dump cart and headed to the orchard where he met his mother picking up sticks. While his mother had worked hard from the moment, she had married his father, he couldn't imagine asking Ginny to clean up an orchard, especially in this cool mist. A north wind blew from across the Lake and Andrew pulled up his collar. No, like Nancy, Ginny was not prepared to assume the constant responsibilities of a farm wife. Such a laborious life would ruin any love Ginny felt for him. Andrew bent over and lifted a limb onto the cart.

As the wind shredded the clouds, the first stars appeared. At the edge of the hay field, Andrew backed up the team, released a lever and dumped the last load of litter. Come winter when snow covered the ground, he would burn the brush pile. Back at the barn, he combed the horses, fed them oats and hay, and headed to the kitchen for a snack.

"A long day." His mother handed Andrew a mug of hot cocoa and a plate of oatmeal raisin cookies. "The temperature's dropping."

"Thanks for your help. I'm sure you're tired." Andrew sipped his cocoa and reached for a cookie.

"Yes, but I'm used to it. I'm sorry about the peaches." His mother stared at her hands. "I don't know why your father bought that land, but we could sell it."

"To some rich man from Chicago so he can build a cottage. Then we would lose our view and access to the Lake. I'd rather cut and split firewood and peddle it in Shorewood." Andrew bit into his third cookie. He would never sell what comforted and sustained him. Through each trial, he had gazed at Lake Michigan and had felt his heartbeat calm and his muscles relax. While the Lake may send storms that destroyed his trees and crop, he would cling to her.

***

In the early morning gloaming, Ginny buttoned her shirtwaist and slipped on a dark-blue linen skirt. If she left now Andrew should be milking. She could return and have the fire lit before her parents awakened. Grabbing a bucket, Ginny strode down the sandy lane. Apricot and lavender melted across the eastern sky as a hermit thrush's silver voice rippled from the small woods by Andrew's farm. When her bare feet stepped on to their farm lane, Ginny gasped.

The first rays of sunlight exposed the raw wood where a peach tree had split or where large branches had snapped off. Hundreds of green peaches freckled the ground along with withering peach leaves. With her heart hammering her ribs, Ginny ran up and down the aisles between the trees as tears wet her cheeks. What had happened? Who would have done this? A tall shadow fell across her path and she whirled around.

"The storm. Wind and hail, and over eight inches of rain fell." Andrew set down his two buckets of milk. "Mother and I cleaned up the worst of the mess last night. I suppose today we should rake up the peaches and cart them away, so they don't rot here."

Ginny longed to wrap her arms around Andrew and comfort him. His shoulders slumped and weariness brushed shadows beneath those eyes that normally brightened when he saw her. She wanted to offer to work beside him and together they would gather the fallen fruit, but her mother had promised away Ginny's afternoon.

"Will you be able to harvest enough peaches to…?" Women should not ask questions about financial matters, but what would this loss of income mean to Andrew and his mother. And hadn't he mentioned something about a debt? How could she help them when her father controlled the family accounts?

"We'll manage. Mother thinks we should sell the sheep pasture to pay the loan, but I hope to keep it."

"I hope so, too." Ginny gazed at the fenced in area where a half-dozen ewes and their lambs grazed. If Andrew sold the pasture, he would lose the path down to the Lake to where they could meet in the evenings.

"Here, let me fill your bucket." Andrew poured milk into her pail. "When you come next on Wednesday, please ask my mother for your milk. She's always in the kitchen around this time."

"All right, but why?" Ginny didn't like how Andrew pressed his lips into a thin line. Why didn't he want to see her?

"I think we need to spend less time together." Andrew stepped back. "You have your world, and I have mine."

"Did my mother talk to you?" Why was Andrew acting this way? Ginny's knuckles whitened as she clasped the bail on the bucket.

"No, I just think this is for the best. Have a pleasant day." Andrew turned away and walked to the stone milk house.

Ginny stomped toward home. Had the losses from the storm befuddled Andrew? Or perhaps his mother had convinced her son to cease flirting with her? Had her parents approached Mrs. McBride and asked her to stop their growing relationship? Ginny wanted to shake Andrew and tell him to ignore what any parent had demanded. He had wed Nancy against her parent's wishes, why wouldn't Andrew ignore society's rules for her sake? She shoved open the screen door and paused. Andrew didn't love her the way he had Nancy. The door snapped shut and swatted her rear end. If he sincerely loved her, he wouldn't have turned away from her.

Perched on the white wicker chair, Ginny shifted her weight. After a month of freedom, her mother had insisted on lacing Ginny into a S shaped corset that rounded her bottom and forced her breasts forward. Her mother had swept up Ginny's hair into a fluffy Gibson Girl bun held in place by tortoise shell combs. When Ginny had turned her head too quickly, the roll had slumped, and her mother had had to repair the arrangement. Ginny lifted her teacup and smiled at Mrs. Sandford, as male voices approached the wrap around porch. Boots clattered up the stairs accompanied by the scent of Bay Rum.

"Good afternoon, Mrs. Madden, and sweet Miss Madden." James shook her hand.

"It is wonderful to see you both here." William squeezed Mrs. Madden's hand and turned to Ginny. "And the fairest of them all." He lifted Ginny's hand and kissed it.

"Oh, how charming." Mrs. Madden laughed, and Mrs. Sandford joined her.

Ginny slid her hand between the folds of her skirt, wanting to scrub away the feel of William's lips on her flesh. Never, while she worked with Andrew had he acted in such a forward manner nor had he tried to kiss her, though she wished he had. Then she could cherish a symbol of his affections as she mourned his betrayal. While walking to the Sandford's cottage, she had promised her mother that she would give William a fair chance at courting her, so why did she feel like a gambler rolling dice?

After the maid removed the last of the china, William turned to Ginny. "Would you like to stroll on the beach? Your mother commented how you walk there in the afternoon."

"With those high waves there isn't much beach, today," Ginny said.

"Nonsense," Mrs. Madden said. "You two would enjoy the wind and the sound of crashing waves. Go on, now." She shooed them away with her hand.

William offered his elbow and Ginny accepted it as they wound down the sandy path edged with dune grass. A few clumps of blue chicory bloomed near a honeysuckle bush with tiny red berries. A wren chattered from the bush and darted inland while overhead large cumulus clouds floated east. The wind tugged at Ginny's hair and she clamped a hand over the bun. A simple braid would have been better for this adventure.

"Let it tumble," William said. "Don't worry, I've seen women with their hair down. And you have lovely hair." He fondled her escaping locks.

Ginny grabbed the locks and poked the combs back into place. Whose hair had William witnessed, his former fiancés' or a woman of the night? Rumors about how William spent his late nights had circled in their society. When she had mentioned the tales to her parents, her father had dismissed them as youthful antics and had ensured her how William had outgrown such activities. He had described William as respectable and reliable, a worthy man who would provide and protect his wife.

"Please call me William, and may I call you Virginia?" William walked beside her as the waves tumbled near his boots.

"I suppose so, but I prefer Ginny." She stepped as far away from William as the narrow beach allowed. They had known each other from early childhood, so such familiarity could be embraced.

"Ginny was fine when you wore pinafores, but it doesn't suit a dignified beautiful woman." William slipped his arm through hers, drawing her closer to him. "My mother told me about your dinner party, and I add my praises. Preparing meals this summer will help when you become a wife and manage a kitchen staff."

Ginny didn't want to be called Virginia. She didn't yearn for a kitchen staff in Chicago, she wanted a certain farmhouse on the lakeshore and the farmer. But the farmer didn't want her. If she did not want to live with her parents for the rest of her life, she would have to marry someone. Spying a lucky stone, Ginny pulled away from William, picked up the tiny pebble, and made a wish Andrew would regret his decision.

"What did you find?" William extended his hand."

"A lucky stone." Ginny dropped it onto his palm. "You make a wish on it."

"Your innocence is refreshing, but I don't need wishes to get what I want." Raising his arm, he threw the lucky stone into the Lake.

"Don't!" Ginny's eyes followed the tiny rock as a wave swallowed it, drowning her wish. Her heart sank as she remembered the loss of Andrew. Even the cry of the seagulls and the sandpipers running along the beach couldn't cheer her. Perhaps her fate demanded a journey along the path her father had prescribed, and for which her mother had prepared her. When William threaded his fingers through hers, she didn't pull away.

"He's here!" Mrs. Madden opened the back porch screen door. "Virginia, please meet our chef, Mr. Francis Chapin."

Thin and wiry, his black hair combed neatly, at six-feet and six-inches, Mr. Chapin towered over Ginny. He wore tweed trousers, and a shirt dotted with little navy-blue anchors. Faint green, blue, and red paint speckled his extended hand while in his other hand he carried a basket of wax beans.

"Pleased to meet you." Ginny shook Mr. Chapin's hand and smiled at his cocoa brown eyes. This fellow couldn't be more than a year older than she was, yet her parents approved of installing him as their chef. He might be willing to allow her to help him prepare dinner and could teach her some tips. After he had cooked for a few days, she would offer her assistance. Ginny yearned to snap the beans into bitesize pieces, steam them and sprinkle them with melted butter and summer savory.

"Thank you so much for hiring me, Mrs. Madden. As a young artist, I dearly appreciate the income. I bought a chicken for this evening's meal. I assume your family likes chicken and dumplings."

"We certainly do. I look forward to dining on your creations. Come along, Ginny. You are no longer needed here."

"Yes, mother." Ginny escaped to the side porch, slipped off her boots, and flopped down in a hammock. She wiggled her toes, wishing she could strip off her stockings. Her mother followed and sat in a wicker rocker. Ginny's shoulders tensed. What had she done wrong this time?

"There's no need for such a sour expression, Virginia. Last night, William asked your father if he may court you, and, of course, Papa said yes. To ensure a favorable impression, you need a better wardrobe. Plus, you ruined several frocks working at that farm."

Ginny would ruin another dress if she could stand on the platform with a spray gun and work with Andrew. And the laundress had removed the strawberry stains from her white shirtwaist. While Ginny would enjoy selecting a few new shirtwaists and skirts, her mother envisioned fancier and more restricting garments.

"We will visit the new seamstress in Saugatuck and list the different sorts of frocks you will need for various social functions, from tea parties to the Maxwell's Summer Ball to informal outings with William. Your father gave him permission to take you canoeing and you may share a picnic."

"Alone? Without a chaperone?" If her parents agreed to the arrangement, why had they fussed about her times with Andrew?

"Yes. William promised his behavior would be beyond reproach."

Ginny would have enjoyed such freedom with Andrew, but William's fingers in her hair had raised gooseflesh on her arms. If he displayed boldness during a walk, what might he attempt while sitting on a blanket?

***

Throwing down his towel, Andrew plunged into the three-foot-high waves and swam out to the sandbar. The sunset burnished the Lake as the sky blazed with red and orange. A few cirrus clouds feathered the sky and blurred the sun. Andrew wished Ginny stood beside him. Throughout the day, he had tried to erase the images of her racing through the peach orchard and weeping over the crippled trees and damaged fruit. Nancy had only walked between the trees when he had escorted her with the offer to pick a perfectly ripe peach. He had licked the peach juice from her chin and lowered her onto a bed of orchard grass. Although she had murmured about discretion, he had unbuttoned her bodice while pulling down her drawers. Nancy had moaned and slid off his trousers. He still believed that moment had created their child.

Heat raced over him. What would it be like to welcome Ginny to the hay mound and inch his lips along her neck? To have Ginny wrap her slender arms around him as he kissed her and ran his tongue inside her mouth. How would she respond as he caressed her rear end? *Stop it*, Andrew chided himself. Today, he had destroyed any chances of seeking her affections and fulfilling his dreams. He should be relieved knowing how he had spared Ginny from a fate like Nancy's. But her dismayed expression haunted him, and her angry stride as she retreated revealed her inner emotions. No, relief didn't dwell inside him, only the resolution to prevent any harm to Ginny.

Andrew swam ashore and dried off. Instead of walking south in the direction of Ginny's cottage, Andrew trudged north toward Pier Cove. His mother had reminded him how Elizabeth and Sarah Martin from their church lived on a farm close to the cove. His mother had said, what better place to discover a wife than on another fruit farm. Now and then during a Sunday service, he had glanced at the twin sisters garbed in white shirtwaists and long black skirts with their brown hair pinned up in buns and then his mind returned to the sermon. But at the first meeting with Ginny, a flame had ignited inside him that must be smothered before it would destroy them.

Chapter Nine

"What are you doing?" Ginny stood in the kitchen doorway, aware of her mother sitting at her desk in the other room. For over a week, she had avoided entering the kitchen while Francis worked, but this afternoon the fragrance of beef barley soup drew her feet to the threshold. She missed the humble tasks of chopping onions and parsley or kneading bread dough. Thankfully, she still scrambled eggs or flipped pancakes for breakfast. But after cleaning up the kitchen, the hours plodded by with endless social calls.

"Sketching while the bread rolls rise and soup simmers." Francis turned the narrow sketch book towards her and exposed a still life composed of a bowl overflowing with green beans. "Do you like to draw?"

"I used to when I attended a ladies' seminary." Ginny had relished the feel of charcoal as she brushed it against the textured paper. Why had she stopped drawing? Because her mother had complained how even after a brisk scrubbing the smudges of gray lingered under Ginny's fingernails. Ginny had suggested buying a set of pastels, but her mother had refused the purchase.

"You should try again. I could buy you a sketchbook." Francis studied her. "Some morning, may I paint you? I'd love to capture the color of your hair."

"I suppose so." Ginny twisted a curl. There wasn't anything improper about having one's portrait painted. "Thank you for the offer. I'd like a sketchbook and some pencils." Perhaps if Ginny skipped using charcoal, her mother would accept the activity.

Standing on the chain ferry, Ginny loved how the morning sunlight shot threads of silver through the rippling current. She longed for her own boat so she could glide down the river, round the tree lined shore and slip onto Lake Michigan. Without the activities of planning meals, going shopping in Douglas, life had lost its structure. When she had arrived at the farm, Andrew's mother had filled her milk bucket and handed her a basket of eggs. Ginny had wanted to ask about Andrew, but Mrs. McBride's expression had stilled her tongue. Maybe sketching would help her pass the time between her mother's arranged social engagements. The ferryman heaved on the crank and the chain rattled as the flatbed boat crossed the Kalamazoo and docked at Water Street.

"This way," Mrs. Madden directed Ginny as they crossed to a small side street, opened a door and a bell jangled. The overpowering perfume of gardenias flooded Ginny's nose and she sneezed. A tall, brown-haired woman wearing a gray linen skirt and crisp white shirtwaist with a lace insertion in the bodice walked through a pair of dark red velvet drapes.

Bolts of satins, silks, poplins, and lawns in a rainbow of colors decorated the shelves along with cards of ribbons and rolls of lace. A wooden chest with numerous drawers filled most of one wall. A dressmaker's dummy wore a fluttering pale blue creation while other frocks hung on hangers. Several large brim hats rested on another shelf and Ginny wanted to try on all of them.

"Good afternoon, Mrs. Madden." The woman extended her hand.

"Good afternoon, Mrs. Rose, please meet my daughter, Virginia Madden." Mrs. Madden nodded at Ginny who shook Mrs. Rose's hand. "As I mentioned, because most of my daughter's wardrobe remains in Chicago, she needs a few summer frocks and a ball gown."

"To hold the attentions of a certain gentleman, I assume?" Mrs. Rose winked at Ginny.

"Please, nothing too fancy." Ginny sneezed, again.

"She needs attire to remind her escort of her delicate femininity," Mrs. Madden said. "Frocks sewn from shear lawns, with ruffles and rows of lace. Like that one." She pointed to the flowing pale blue dress with three-quarter sleeves edged with lace.

"Would you like to try it on?" Mrs. Rose reached for the gown. "There's a dressing room in the back. Come this way, please."

After Mrs. Rose unbuttoned the back of Ginny's shirt waist, she guided the gossamer frock over Ginny's head, chattering about how the color flattered her smooth pink cheeks. Ginny was thankful her mother had remained in the shop, pawing through gloves, eying lacy drawers, and gored petticoats with large dust ruffles.

"The frock shows off your slim figure and your bust fills the bodice well. Aren't these new corsets wonderful? Wives had told me that their husbands love how they emphasize a woman's round rear end." Mrs. Rose fussed with the skirt. "What do you think?"

Ginny stared at the mirror. The lace insertion in the bodice hinted at what was hidden beneath the fragile fabric and the sleeves exposed her wrists. What would Andrew think of her this frock? She turned and gazed at her profile. Yes, the new corsets and slimmer petticoats revealed more of a woman's rear end. Were these contraptions inspired by men for their pleasure or for a woman's welfare? Her mother parted the curtains.

"Aren't you stunning! You must wear this when you attend the Mitchell's garden party with…" Mrs. Madden covered her mouth. "We'll order two more, one in white and one in light pink, please. Now for the ball gown."

Mrs. Madden and Mrs. Rose studied illustrations in a lady's fashion magazine as Ginny tried on several hats. While her spirit ached at how the two older women wanted to mold her into a fashionable young lady, she enjoyed the lovely creations with wide brims decorated with feathers and silk flowers. She pinned on a light blue velvet hat trimmed with a dark blue ribbon and a wreath of pale pink rose buds. Ginny's mother smiled at her.

"Utterly charming. Feminine and innocently appealing. Please add that wonderful hat to our bill. Virginia, what do you think of this gown?" Her mother turned the magazine so she could see the illustration.

A sage-green silk skirt with two ruffles of black lace was attached to a scoop necked bodice sewn from pale green lace. A lacy ruffle sprinkled with embroidered rosebuds fell across the bodice, so it brushed the tops of the woman's bosom and her shoulders where small-capped sleeves ended above the elbows.

"It's beautiful." Ginny longed to watch Andrew's expression as he watched her gliding toward him in the gown. Would his eyes widen? Would he catch his breath and slip his arms around her? For Andrew, she would enjoy wearing these clothes, and yet might they remind him of Nancy and the distance between their classes?

"Please begin sewing it, Mrs. Rose," Ginny's mother said. "Add the cost of the silk and lace to my bill. We will need it for next month's ball."

William, not Andrew would witness her in this gown. She would become a decoration to entice him, yet Ginny must remain chase and refuse even a kiss. The hypocrisy of the game of courtship dug a pit in her stomach. What was wrong with her that she had never yearned to engage in the rituals the way her Chicago friends did?

After departing the seamstress' shop, Ginny guided her mother to the two-story white clapboard Riverside Hotel with a flat roof. Green trim framed the numerous windows and a screened in porch ran along the front of the building. Standing outside with his easel, Francis painted with watercolors. Four other men and two women also worked on either oil or watercolor paintings. Both women had pinned small purple ribbons to their shirtwaists. One of the women wore a white shirtwaist tucked into gray bloomers reaching down to her calves, revealing her black stockings. Ginny's mother's face reddened at the sight. Francis set his brush into a small bucket of gray water.

"Thank you for coming! I have your sketchbook." He shook their hands and introduced his friends who nodded at them. "Let me fetch it and some pencils."

While Francis dashed to his room, Ginny gazed at the different paintings. Although each person painted the blue hydrangea bushes bordering the wide porch their styles differed. One man had blurred the flowers as if they melted into each other while another replicated each petal. The woman in bloomers threw her brush into her little bucket filled with murky water.

"Someone please tell me what I am doing wrong? I can't capture how those flowers make me feel."

"Maybe you should sketch them first," the other woman said. "Maybe you need to understand their anatomy like when we draw nudes."

Ginny blushed. These women had sat in front of a person with no clothes on and drawn them? What type of person would disrobe for a group of artists? When her family had visited the Chicago Institute of Art, her mother had whisked her by any paintings with nude images. Boots clattered on the hotel's steps and Francis extended a package wrapped in brown paper.

"Here you, go. You can add the cost of it and the pencils to my next pay."

"Thank you so much." Ginny tucked the book under her arm. "Might you provide a few lessons, too?"

"I don't think you will have much time for them," Mrs. Madden said. "Our social schedule is filling quickly."

"If you leave your sketch book in the kitchen, I can make a few comments and suggestions," Francis said. "Mrs. Madden, which would you rather have for dinner tonight, white fish or trout?"

"The white fish, please. We must go, Virginia." Mrs. Madden slipped her arm through Ginny's and tugged her toward the ferry.

"Yes, mother." Ginny removed her arm and strode along the street. One minute her mother treated her as a grown woman to auction off and the next she was a child to be dragged home. She needed to become more like the young woman wearing bloomers.

***

Andrew slit the envelope and unfolded the letter.

Dear Mr. McBride,

We were sorry to read about the arrival of this new pest to your orchard. We have not named the moth yet but are researching its life cycle. In the meantime, the only solution to the problem is to cut off the tips of every limb where you see dying leaves. We think the larva lives in the end of the branches. Then burn these trimmings. Sincerely, Dr. James Miller

He needed to head to the orchard and begin trimming those branches. Andrew marched to the barn and pulled out a pair of pruning shears and a couple of bushel baskets. If he had to work by the light of the moon, he would finish this job tonight. His mother's shadow filled the doorway.

"Andrew, have you forgotten the box social? We're raising funds for more desks and other items for the school. We need to be there by six." His mother shook her head. "The twins are counting on you."

He closed his eyes. Blast it all, if the local girls were attuned to farm life, then they would understand a farmer's need to complete this task as soon as possible. But it was no use arguing with his mother. Andrew set down the shears and trudged to the house.

A half-an-hour later, Andrew escorted his mother into the two-story, white clapboard Union School built on Douglas' main street. Throughout his education, Andrew had studied in each of the four classrooms as he proceeded from first to twelfth grade. He had not earned the marks of an exceptional student, but his achievements had prepared him for farming and given him a love of reading. Before the death of their infant had sent Nancy into a melancholy state, he had read to her each night before they went to bed. Now, most nights he read a few minutes to calm his mind and to erase his thoughts of Ginny. What sort of books did she enjoy?

"The boxes are in this classroom," his mother said, and they turned right.

Several maps of the United States, Europe and the rest of the world decorated the cream-colored walls. And each classroom also featured a photograph of President

Woodrow Wilson and framed prints of Presidents George Washington and Abraham Lincoln. The desks had been lined up against one wall and light from the tall windows illuminated the table with the boxes. A group of men circled the display, chatting and teasing each other.

Andrew's thick sole boots thumped on the wooden floor and he ran a finger around his tight collar as he examined the decorated boxes. Wallpaper covered many of them along with pasted on ribbons, a few seashells and silk flowers. How was he supposed to know which ones the twins had created? Even if he could discern the girls' boxes, he couldn't bid on both as he wasn't going to turn into a Mormon. How he wished Ginny had filled a box and slipped it onto the table. His intuition would alert him to her offering and after buying it, they could eat supper together. His mother nudged his elbow.

"Sarah and Elizabeth made those two." She nodded her head.

"Well, I can't bid on both of them." He would try for the blue one as it reminded him of Ginny's eyes.

"The girls will understand. But you must buy one of them." His mother's skirt swished across the floor as she walked to a cluster of friends.

"I was sorry to hear about Nancy," Tom Campbell said. "Such a tragic loss."

"Thank you." Andrew rubbed his chin. How much did folks know about Nancy's suicide? What would the locals think about him courting so soon after her death?

"I suppose it's hard to run a farm without a wife," Tom said. "Of course, these young ladies should think about how their future husbands might end up fighting in Germany."

"Do you think Wilson will send us to war?" Andrew hoped America wouldn't become involved in England's battles.

"I hope not. But the situation is risky."

"Ladies and gentlemen, please gather around so we can start the bidding," Mr. Johnson the high school teacher called, and the crowd quieted.

"Who will bid ten cents for this lovely creation?" He held up a box covered in wallpaper with ivy running across the sides. With a white ribbon, the lady had tied on sprigs of real ivy.

"I will," Tom called, and another man outbid him. The bids rose by pennies until Tom shouted out, "One dollar!" Tom looked about the room and Anne Butler walked over to him.

Box by box, the teacher cajoled the men to not hurt the young ladies' feelings who had invested time decorating their containers and filling them with delicious food. Once, he sniffed a box and declared how he smelled apple pie in it. After each sale, one of the girls would join the fellow who had bought her creation. Finally, he held out one of the twin's boxes.

"A delicate young lady must have created this one as she loves pink." Pale pink wallpaper dotted with sprays of dark pink roses flowed over the container, tied with a pale blue ribbon. A bouquet of maroon and white roses adorned the lid.

"Twenty-five cents," Andrew said, and another man countered him. At seventy-five cents, Andrew stopped bidding. As the fellow claimed the box, Sarah accepted his elbow.

Andrew cracked his knuckles. No matter what the price, he had to buy the other box, or his mother would chide him for the rest of the week. He didn't mind contributing to the school fund, but the loss of so many peaches meant fewer nickels to spend on frivolity. He shouldn't think such thoughts, but Elizabeth should understand the challenges of farming.

"Ten cents!" Andrew said and the bidding climbed between him and two other men. Finally, Andrew shouted, "One dollar and ten cents!"

As the older women twittered, Elizabeth's cheeks blushed. The other bidders shook their heads and stepped back. Andrew handed the teacher the correct sum, and Elizabeth walked to him.

"Thank you. I've never made a box that brought the highest bid." Elizabeth smiled up at him. "I brought a tablecloth so we could have a picnic."

"It is a beautiful box and I'm sure you cooked a fine surprise." Andrew gave her his arm and led Elizabeth to the edge of the small rise where they could look out over Silver Lake.

They spread the blue and white checked tablecloth and settled on it. Elizabeth unpacked three meat pies, several bread rolls, butter, coleslaw, stuffed eggs, dill pickles, and two cupcakes with chocolate frosting and a quart of lemonade.

"You'll say a blessing?" Elizabeth bowed her head.

As Andrew prayed, he didn't shut his eyes but gazed at Elizabeth's glowing face, shining brown hair, and turned up nose. While the girl lacked Ginny's curls and plentiful bosom, Elizabeth was pretty in an innocent way. Her hands were stronger looking than Ginny's. Her feet were larger, too. Elizabeth's figure didn't draw men's eyes like Ginny's, yet the lass filled out her shirtwaist in a pleasing way. Sturdy was the word his mother had used to describe Elizabeth, but Andrew would rather think of the girl as refreshing. He finished the blessing and reached for a plate.

"Excellent meat pies." Andrew took another bite. Now what should he say? Elizabeth was quieter than himself.

"Thank you. My grandmother brought the recipe from Wales." Elizabeth dabbed her mouth with a napkin.

"So, you're Welsh?" Andrew sipped his lemonade before consuming a stuffed egg. The girl knew how to cook, unless her mother helped her. He took another dill pickle. "You made these?"

"Yes. My father is from Wales." She glanced at him. "But my mother's English. They immigrated as children."

"Most of our parents came from somewhere else. What matters is how they lived their lives and what they taught us." Andrew couldn't believe he had made that statement. Elizabeth's shoulders relaxed. Perhaps he needed to think about his words because from what Ginny had said, her father cared more about making money than how he could use his wealth to help the less fortunate of Chicago. Whereas Elizabeth's parents had bought land and planted orchards just like his folks.

"Cupcake?" Elizabeth held out the cake mounded with frosting.

Andrew's fingers touched hers as he accepted the treat. "Thank you."

Chapter Ten

Dressed in a tan linen skirt and a sheer, white shirtwaist with a pleated front, Ginny packed the chicken salad sandwiches into a deep wicker basket, added a quart of lemonade and a saucer stacked with frosted brownies. Cucumber spears and carrot strips filled a glass mason jar. The screen door opened, Francis walked into the kitchen and set down a bucket.

"Excited? Looks like you created a wonderful feast." He pulled a white apron off a hook and tied it on.

"My mother asked William's mother what his favorite foods were." Ginny covered the basket's contents with a red checked tablecloth. While she wanted to tell Francis how she would rather spend the afternoon with Andrew, she didn't need him saying anything to her mother.

"I see." Francis pulled a large slab of fish wrapped in paper from his bucket and stored it in the ice box.

"Why did those two women pin little purple ribbons to their shirtwaists?" Ginny played with the tablecloth, tucking it further into the basket. "And are both men and women in the same room when you sketch models?"

She couldn't bring herself to add the word nude. While it was a natural state, it wouldn't be proper for a young lady to mention it. Ginny doubted if she could participate in such a sketching session, and yet she would like to be part of the creative community she had witnessed at the hotel. What would her mother say if Ginny adopted such a life? What would William think?

"The purple ribbons represent the battle for women to earn the right to vote. Those two women have marched in Chicago for the movement. As for nude models, yes, we sit in the same room." Francis glanced at her. "Did you want to visit one of those sessions?"

Ginny's cheeks flamed. "I don't think so. I'd probably drop my pencil."

"I understand. The first time a woman cast aside her robe, I had a hard time concentrating. But when I learned how she was a fellow artist in need of a way to make money, I relaxed. Drawing a nude shows the different ways light shades and emphasizes the anatomy."

"Virginia!" Her mother called. "William is here."

"Have fun." Francis nodded.

Wearing a straw boater and linen suit, William stood on the side porch chatting with Ginny's mother. "I've rented a small sailboat so we can skim along the shoreline."

"How splendid. What a lovely way to spend the afternoon," Mrs. Madden said.

What if she didn't want to be tucked into a sailboat with William? How could her mother send her off without a chaperone? Ginny pinned on a white straw hat with a band of blue running around the edge of the brim and another around the crest of the crown. Yellow silk roses shimmered against a blue ribbon.

"Isn't she charming?" Her mother touched William's arm. "Virginia wanted to surprise you with this new shirtwaist. Aren't the pleats sweet? And the little ruffles?"

Ginny bit her tongue. Sweet wasn't the word she would have chosen. The thin fabric made the pleats emphasize her bosom along with the ruffles framing each side of the front of the shirtwaist. Whoever had created the design wasn't thinking about modesty.

"Yes, lovelier than any flower." William's gaze lingered on her curves as he reached for the picnic basket.

"Now don't forget, you two, that Mr. Madden is lounging on the beach with his spy glass." Mrs. Madden laughed. "Enjoy yourselves."

While he might behave himself close to their cottage, what if William sailed out of sight of the spyglass? Did her mother know of William's reputation or had she chosen to ignore it? William slid his arm through hers and guided her to the door. Why did Ginny feel like a minnow swimming into a trap? She freed her arm and lifted the edges of her skirt so it wouldn't drag on the wooden porch steps.

"The boat is tied up at our place." William took her hand. "I thought we would sail to the mouth of the Kalamazoo and find a picnic spot."

Ginny attempted to pull her hand away, but William clasped it firmly until they reached the sailboat where the family's handyman met them. William placed the basket in the hull and helped Ginny settle on a seat.

"You two get in and I'll push you off," the man said as William sat near the rudder.

The handy man shoved, and the boat rocked as it slid into the low waves. Ginny clutched the seat. While each spring she looked forward to the homecoming boat trip down the Kalamazoo River, she had never sailed on Lake Michigan. Tales of shipwrecks and drownings seeped into her mind.

"We will stay close to shore?" How well could she swim in these clothes? If they sailed in shallow water, she could walk out of the Lake.

William laughed. "Of course not! Time for a little adventure." He stared out past the sandbar and the boom swung around as he aimed for deeper water. The waves slapped the boat sending it up and down. Ginny swallowed down bile. She had never experienced sea sickness on the river, but her stomach roiled. She closed her eyes. She would not mortify herself in front of William.

"Please go back. I don't feel well." Bile slicked her tongue and her palms had turned clammy. "Please, William."

"Certainly, for the price of a kiss." William leaned forward. "And not a little peck, my sweet."

Ginny longed to slap William, but she had to get out of the boat. Scooting forward to the edge of the seat, she pursed her lips and closed her eyes. Strong hands reached for her as William clasped her waist and pulled her onto his lap. She twisted, but his hands clamped her against his thighs and his elbows pinned her arms.

"Not until you give…." His lips smothered hers as William pressed harder and longer. His tongue pried open her mouth and roamed the inside.

When she struggled, he pinched her. Ginny gasped. Andrew had never taken such liberties, nor would he hurt her. She pushed against William's chest and kicked her feet, and the boat pitched up and down.

"That's not a good idea." William rubbed his cheek against hers. "We will leave when I am finished. I've longed for this moment for days. And if someone sees us, what will they think of *you* sitting on my lap? Come now." William's mouth covered hers again.

Ginny hated him. Hated how even with two petticoats and her drawers, she could feel him swelling. William groaned and pressed her rear end against him. Ginny and her friends had imagined the rituals of their future wedding nights, but never had she imagined this odd dance as William rocked back and forth. If she tried to slide off him, would she cause the boat to overturn? He gasped and fell back against the stern. Through his half-opened eyes, he smirked. A wetness stained the front of his trousers and a dampness seeped through her skirt. Ginny jumped back to her seat and the boat leaned to one side. Perhaps it should capsize and drown her mortification.

"I told you I always get what I want. If you tattle to your father, he won't believe you, and your mother would start planning our wedding to ensure your reputation remains pure."

"I'll never marry you!" Ginny would drown in the Lake before taking this man's name. Why was he so keen on wedding her?

William laughed. "Remember, I *always* get what I want. Be glad you aren't one of our maids. Even if they lock their doors, I have the spare keys."

She yearned to scrub her body and her rear end ached from where William had pounded her. Was the back of her skirt stained? How could he use her like that? Why would her father not defend her? After this encounter, was marriage the only solution? Tears trickled down her cheeks. Why had her parents allowed them to be alone?

"I'm famished. Where should we eat our picnic so the world can watch a sweet courting couple?" William steered the boat towards the beach.

"I'm not hungry." Ginny wiped her tears. How could William think about food? She wouldn't be able to eat for a week. Nothing but tea and toast.

"But your future husband is. How about on that small knoll?" William kicked off his boots, jumped and hauled the boat onto the beach. He offered Ginny his hand, but she swatted it away, and grabbed the basket. His eyes glinted.

"Take my hand or every single male in Shorewood will hear how you unbuttoned your drawers and begged for more."

Ginny slid her trembling fingers through William's, and he led her into the dunes.

Back at the cottage, Ginny thumped the picnic basket down on the kitchen table and Francis glanced at her.

"He was that bad? Bye, bye William." Francis snapped the ends off a green bean. "I admit, I prefer your farmer friend."

"I wish." Ginny ran out the back door, stripped off her boots and stockings and dashed down the path. She jumped onto the beach and threw herself in the water. Her father shouted at her, but she kicked her legs and swam to the sandbar. Thankfully, no one else stood on the narrow strip of sand. With her palms, she scrubbed her face and arms until her skin stung. Taking off her skirt, she examined the stained back. She would toss it in the rubbish along with everything else covering her. But how could she cast William from her life? Throwing back her head, she sobbed, willing the sensation of William pounding against her to flow away in the water. She longed to confide to someone, to pour out her shame and guilt and ask questions. What if she found herself in the family way? What would she do? She must ensure William never caught her alone, again.

***

Andrew hung up his suit, threw his shirt onto his bed and pulled on work clothes. Staring at the sleigh bed, thoughts of Nancy tumbled through him. Until the death of their child, she had

teased him at bedtime or she had kissed him awake in the wee hours of the night so they could enact her lusty dream. She hadn't been an ideal farm wife, but Nancy had provided hours of pleasures. Heat poured over him and he yearned for those nights. If he married quiet Elizabeth, would she surprise him or would she view their bed as part of her wifely duties? Ginny showed enough passion in living to display how she would behave between the sheets. Andrew inhaled as he envisioned unbuttoning her shirtwaist and sliding it off her shoulders.

"Blast it all." Andrew tied up his work boots. He didn't have time for women and needed to concentrate on his peach trees. They had to regain their vigor so they could give their energy to growing and ripening their peaches.

Out in the orchard, Andrew cut off the tips of the branches with withered leaves and dropped them into a bushel basket. With each cut the mound of leaves grew and Andrew tried to push aside the pain expanding inside him. Between the moths and the storm, how many peaches would remain? How would they repay their loan? The bank had already allowed them a six- month grace period. He wished Ginny worked beside him, chattering, and cheering his spirit. Instead, a mourning dove cooed as the sun slid closer to the Lake and mare's tails clouds rippled across the sky. Andrew worked until bats darted over the trees. Even though the peaches were the size of plums, their fuzz had floated onto Andrew's face, neck, and back. He didn't care if someone saw him in his union suit. Tucking his pruning shears next to the basket, he ran down the dune, stripped off his shirt and trousers, and dove into the Lake.

Bliss, pure bliss. The waves washed away the fuzz, the heat, and relaxed his muscles. Why had he agreed to his mother inviting Elizabeth to dinner on Saturday? Because he was supposed to be courting her. Perhaps he should try kissing her and see how she responded. But such an action would indicate serious intentions, and was he serious?

Andrew floated on his back, staring up at the darkening sky as stars emerged and glittered. What should he do about the pasture? He didn't want to sell it. But his mother had pointed out how they could write into the agreement the right to have access to the beach. That might work with the first buyer, but what if that person sold the land to someone unwilling to allow Andrew to tramp across his lawn? Anyone who bought the property would build a house and destroy Andrew's view of the Lake. While the thought flooded him with sadness, his mother couldn't understand his need for beautiful landscapes. He seldom spotted her watching how the sunlight flitted across the waves or appreciating the hues of a sunset. She insisted that selling the sheep pasture was the best solution to discharging their debt and for providing a small cushion for the winter months. Andrew hoped she was wrong.

Chapter Eleven

Ginny served her parents bowls of oatmeal with raisins, set down a plate of toast, and settled into her chair. After last night's scolding by her mother about ruining her clothes, Ginny didn't expect any pleasant breakfast conversations. Her father had shaken his head and muttered about women and had headed out to smoke cigars with Mr. Mitchell. Now he opened *The Chicago Tribune* and read aloud the news about the war in Europe.

"Please, Mr. Madden, I am not ready to hear about battles this early in the morning," her mother said and dipped her spoon in to her oatmeal.

"Mark my words, at some point our country will have to enter into the conflict." Mr. Madden sipped his coffee.

"I hope not. Virginia don't forget that we have a ten o'clock appointment with the dressmaker. Did you and William set a day for your next outing?"

"No." Ginny buttered her toast. If she could figure out a way, she would avoid William for the rest of her life. How could she stay in Douglas and not return to Chicago where William's family dominated society?

"Well, I'll drop some hints to his mother." Mrs. Madden sipped her tea. "Perhaps he could escort you to Sunday's band concert."

"Only if we are properly chaperoned or attend with several other couples." Ginny stared at her mother. "I refuse to be left alone with William." In her lap, her hands balled up her napkin.

"Oh?" Her mother lifted her eyebrows and glanced at her father.

"He's much too forward." Ginny's cheeks flushed as her body remembered William rocking beneath her.

Her father laughed. "He's a young man. You are a beautiful woman. Of course, he will press you for a kiss or two." He reached over and squeezed his wife's hand. "Your mother understood my needs and found my kisses pleasing."

"Mr. Madden! We avoided any serious misconduct. I'm sure, Virginia, you are making too much over William's attentions."

No, she wasn't, but if neither of her parents would listen to her, who would? Why did the image of Andrew slamming his fist into William's jaw emerge in her mind? She needed to think how to defend herself against further unwanted advances.

Ginny stood in the dressmaker's shop as Mrs. Rose adjusted the ball gown at the waist and pinned the bodice, so it molded to Ginny's bosom. After the episode in the sailboat the hypocrisy of society roiled her stomach, encouraging woman's clothing to entice young men, teaching girls to remain chase, and then looking aside when a man forced himself upon a woman. Ginny yearned to shake her parents out of their complacency. Were stocks and prestige worth sacrificing their daughter? Most of all, why was William so determined to marry her when other girls would race into his arms? Did he see her as a quest? A mountain to climb and claim?

"If your gentleman doesn't propose after viewing you in this frock, I won't charge you for my labor." Mrs. Rose laughed.

"Oh, I'm sure he will and then you can design Virginia's wedding gown." Mrs. Madden hummed a classical melody played at weddings. "Relax your shoulders, dear, so Mrs. Rose can adjust the ruffle. I love how it brushes her bosom."

"Yes, a reminder of what is hidden." Mrs. Rose fluffed the black lace. "And you fill out the bodice in a delicious way."

"Thank you. When we are finished, may we please walk by the artists? I'd like to see what they are painting." Ginny glanced at her mother, hoping that by asking in front of Mrs. Rose, her mother would agree to the request.

"I suppose so. Francis suggested you would like to visit them."

Thank heavens for Francis's intervention. While Ginny hadn't wanted him in her kitchen, the fellow understood her better than her parents and could influence them for her. Should she ask him about how to handle William?

Ginny and her mother strolled to the Riverside Hotel where the same group of artists plus another man and a woman painted by the edge of the river. Laughter rippled from the group as someone made a comment. She should have brought her sketch book and joined them. Scenes of the Kalamazoo were spread across their canvasses and watercolor paper. The artists had captured how the sunlight threaded through the current, the ducks swimming near the docks, and the chain ferry posed halfway across the river. Cottages and homes, fishing shanties and the cruise ship from Chicago illustrated the common activities of Saugatuck.

"I don't know why you like to come here," her mother whispered. "You have fifteen minutes. We're having lunch at the Mitchell's in an hour."

Ginny ambled around the edge of the half-circle of artists studying the paintings until the woman in bloomers recognized her.

"Your Francis' friend. How's the sketching going?" Today she sported a brown pair of bloomers with a cream-colored shirtwaist. "I'm Margaret but everyone calls me Maggie."

"I'm having fun, but I'm not good at it. I'm Ginny." She offered her hand. "I probably could use some lessons."

"I'm Anne. Please, come join us tomorrow," the other woman said and shook Ginny's hand. Her brown hair was tucked beneath a narrow-brimmed straw hat, and she wore navy-blue bloomers and a purple ribbon pinned to her shirtwaist. "We're all at different skill levels. I'm learning about watercolors this summer. We could give you some tips."

"Thank you, I'll see what I can do. I like your purple pin."

"Here, I have more." Anne removed it and pinned it on Ginny's shirtwaist. "Someday soon, we'll have the right to vote."

"Thank you." Ginny glanced at her frowning mother. "I had better go." What a conundrum, wearing a symbol for women's suffrage while attached to her mother's side. Ginny loved her mother, but she needed to declare her independence before…. Before what?

"What is that." Her mother pointed at the purple ribbon.

"A symbol of women's suffrage." Ginny lifted her chin. "I hope to have the right to vote."

"And why would you need to vote? Your husband will make those decisions. Take that silly pin off." Her mother walked toward the ferry.

"That woman over there is wearing one, too." Ginny nodded her head at a woman leaving a shop. Glancing around, Ginny noticed several other women with either purple or white ribbons pinned to their shirtwaists.

"We do not believe in the unfeminine behavior of the suffragettes. Their husbands and ministers should remind them of their womanly duties to bless their homes."

"Why couldn't a woman fulfill those duties and still vote?" Something bubbled up in Ginny, like yeast expanding flour and water, she snatched at the desire to vote and express her own opinions.

"William nor any other gentleman would never approve of such…such boldness. When you take William's name and come under his protection and authority, you will wipe away such ideas and demure to his leading."

Ginny's eyes glinted over the irony of the idea of William protecting her. Perhaps she didn't want to marry any man at this point. Let alone obey him. She wanted to separate herself from the rules of society, and to help create new expectations and opportunities for women.

***

As Elizabeth's voice floated up the stairs, Andrew pulled on a clean shirt and combed back his damp hair. He should change into clean trousers, but he didn't have time for switching his suspenders to a different pair of pants. He rushed down the stairs.

"Good evening, Elizabeth. Sorry I'm a little behind." Andrew escorted her into the dining room and pulled out her chair.

His mother had spread a clean tablecloth edged with red-cross stitch embroidery and had set out her best china. Wreaths of blue and pink flowers circled the plates and the small fruit bowls. His grandmother McBride's silverware shone against the linen tablecloth as did the water goblets. From her garden, his mother had picked a large bouquet of multicolored zinnias. Andrew pushed in Elizabeth's chair and then seated his mother.

"Please say a blessing." His mother bowed her head.

While Andrew prayed, his eyes ran over Elizabeth's hair pinned into an attractive chiffon that softened her face, and her calico shirtwaist tucked into a gored skirt emphasized her curves and narrow waist. Had she created the chiffon to please him? Perhaps she was serious about courting. He needed to respond, but with what? Andrew closed the prayer and spread his napkin.

His mother kept the conversation flowing until they scraped the last chocolate cake crumbs and smidges of frosting from their plates. When she turned the topic onto preserving the garden, Elizabeth sighed,

"I will be thankful to finish that chore. And we still have pears to can," Elizabeth said.

"Yes, but this winter our families will enjoy a full pantry and root cellar." Mrs. MacBride folded her napkin. "You two go for a stroll and I'll clean up. No need to help."

Andrew offered Elizabeth his arm. "Would you like to walk on the beach and watch the sun set?"

"No thank you. I hate getting sand in my shoes. It's so frustrating to have to stop every few steps and empty them."

"How about a tour of the orchards?" Andrew guided Elizabeth to the rows of trees. "I love how the ripe peaches glow in the late sun."

"Yes, they are pretty. It looks like the storm wrecked several of your trees." Elizabeth watched the ground as they ambled down the rows.

"Yes. I'll have to replant those spots in the spring." Andrew watched Elizabeth's face, but she showed no sympathy for the lost trees. The image of Ginny weeping over the ravaged orchard pricked him.

"That's the trouble with farming. You never know what calamity will strike next." Elizabeth looked up at the cumulus clouds drifting east. "I hope it doesn't rain tomorrow."

"Me, too. If you are available, would you like to go for a ride tomorrow?" Andrew's mother had asked the McVea's if he could borrow their buggy for the afternoon. The lack of a buggy whittled away at his manliness but paying off their debt was more important.

"I am sorry, but my family is going to visit my great-aunt in Fennville after church."

"I'm sure she will appreciate your company. What do you think of the sunset?" Andrew paused and pointed at the orange sky.

Low waves shimmered, reflecting the bronze sun as its rays spread across them. A few gulls floated on the water and a sailboat headed towards the mouth of the Kalamazoo River. Andrew would never lose his love for the countless blending of colors and images as the sun departed. A wood thrush's call floated from the woods and an ache rippled through Andrew.

"I think I better go." Elizabeth nodded at deepening shadows.

"Let me walk you home." Andrew led her down the lane and along the sandy road.

Over the half-mile, they never spoke. Andrew missed Ginny explaining her thoughts or asking him questions. At the end of Elizabeth's lane, he took her hand, wondering if he should attempt to kiss her. If he did, would she think him forward? If he didn't, would she think him uninterested? He waited for her to lift her face as a sign of encouragement.

"Thank you for a lovely evening. Please thank your mother for a wonderful meal." Elizabeth dropped his hand and walked up the path to her house.

Relief trickled over him. Elizabeth was not the girl he yearned to kiss. Trudging home, Andrew pulled open the screen door and found his mother knitting in the kitchen. More lines created wrinkles at the edges of her eyes and the wind had chapped her lips. Since his father's death, her hair had turned gray.

"How did it go?" She looked up. "She's a lovely girl."

"Yes. I'm tired. Good night." Andrew plodded up the stairs. He was weary of plotting mothers who thought they knew whom their offspring should marry.

***

Ginny tapped her croquet ball with her mallet, and it rolled through the wicket and headed towards a clump of ferns. Clusters of lilac bushes hedged the small yard with a gravel path meandering through it, and from a small oak tree, a robin sang. At various locations around the lawn, the three Mitchell sisters stood by their balls. Dressed in white muslin frocks and wide straw hats, they held mallets striped with different colors. Only Ginny had a small purple ribbon pinned to the bodice of her white eyelet dress.

"So, have you enjoyed your times with William?" Lucy asked as she sent her ball through a wicket and onward to the next one.

Should Ginny speak honestly? If she did, would the girls gossip about her? Ginny shifted her weight and wished she could go barefoot. The mowed grass looked soft and would cool her feet. A sudden gust of wind tugged at her hat and she grabbed the brim. Certainly, the sisters knew about William's reputation.

"I felt uncomfortable and was thankful when I could go home." Ginny's eyes followed Beth's ball as it struck Lucy's off course.

"So, once again, William forced himself." Beth glanced at Ginny. "I had to stomp on his toes to break free."

"Someone should write on his forehead, LECHER." Katie struck her ball, and it flew forward. "I hate dancing with him because his hands wander."

Ginny bit her lower lip. As sisters, they could share and keep their secrets, but she couldn't risk her story becoming gossip. Her last two outings with William had been to social events where they mingled with other families from Shorewood. He had to satisfy himself with holding her arm, but still, his fingers had brushed her breast. Although they hadn't announced an engagement, William already controlled her life and she hated him for it.

"Your turn, Ginny," Lucy said. "I doubt if you are daydreaming about William. Perhaps you still fancy that farmer? Your poor mother told my mother how he had you *working* on his farm. How did he trick you into it?"

Ginny's cheeks flushed. "Andrew didn't trick me. I offered to help." Grabbing her ball from the ferns, she placed it near the wicket and whacked it. The red ball bounced over the lawn and landed on the gravel path. Why didn't these girls have the urge for some greater purpose than to marry a wealthy man and produce an heir?

"I see." Beth glanced at her sisters. "He is handsome, but William won't make you work."

William wouldn't allow her to work in the kitchen, or to sweep the floor or to enjoy the daily tasks of homemaking. But he would make her work in the bedroom or wherever he wanted her body. Wearing the outfits William chose, she would have to work to still her tongue at dinner parties and not talk about women's suffrage. Ginny would rather scrub peach fuzz off her neck and smell that sulfur spray in her hair than become William's plaything and baby maker. The click of wooden balls as they hit each other reached Ginny's ears.

"Your turn again," Katie said. "So, tell us, please, why you keep wearing that purple ribbon? Do you really believe in that nonsense or think William would allow you to vote?"

"Yes, I do want to vote. And I haven't married William, yet." Ginny leaned her mallet against a wooden garden bench. "I have a headache." She marched along the dirt road meandering through Shorewood, slipped onto the thin path running along the ridge of the dune, and rushed into her cottage. She slumped into her rocker on the side porch, and Francis stuck his head through the doorway.

"I could hear you sigh from in here. William again?" He dried his hands on his apron. A few dots of paint freckled his neck. From the kitchen floated the fragrance of chicken pot pie.

Ginny's stomached growled. She was supposed to eat a luncheon with the Mitchells. "No, thank God. The Mitchell sisters badgered me about Andrew and helping on his farm. How come no one will believe that I enjoyed it?"

"I do. Anne does, too. In fact, she would like to paint his orchard. Those silly sisters have never questioned how they were raised, and what they were raised for."

"So why do I ask so many questions?" Ginny fiddled with the little purple ribbon.

"Because you are who you are. How about a slice of warm bread? Want to snap some beans?"

"Yes. To both." Ginny followed Francis. Perhaps the repeated motions of preparing the beans would settle her mind.

***

"These are good." Andrew bit into another oatmeal raisin cookie and smiled at Elizabeth. "Even better than my mother's."

"Watch your words." His mother nibbled on a cookie. "You are a serious contender for a blue ribbon at the fair."

"Thank you. I hope someday to win a few ribbons." She gazed at Andrew. "I wanted you to know that I accepted a job as a cook for the next few weeks at a cottage in Shorewood."

"Congratulations." Andrew wondered how her father and mother could spare their daughter during one of the busiest months on the farm and in the garden. A prickle of concern jabbed him. Maybe Elizabeth didn't like farm life?

"I want to build a nest egg." Elizabeth drank the last of her lemonade. "I'd better go home and pack."

"So, you'll live with the family?" his mother asked.

"Yes, it's the only way I can manage to prepare breakfast on time. Plus, if they have dinner parties, I'll work until late."

"Sounds like I won't be able to see you except on Sundays," Andrew said.

"I will have to work on Sundays, too." Elizabeth's hand pushed open the screen door. "Have a wonderful day." Her skirts swished down the back porch steps and her violet perfume faded.

"I had a feeling this might happen." His mother covered the plate of cookies with another plate. "Every time you arrived home from a buggy ride or walk, you were downcast.

"I suppose I should have bought Sarah's box." Andrew ran a hand through his hair. "She's home helping her mother." But what young woman would want to be a man's obvious second choice? And if she knew anything about his relationship with Ginny, then she would see herself as his third choice.

Ginny. He longed to hear her voice and see how her eyes sparkled when she gazed at the orchard. The one evening spent working with the trees had stitched a slim bond between Ginny and the farm. This evening was her time to come for milk. What would it hurt to be the one who filled her container? The lakeshore gossips had whispered about how Ginny had talked to the artists from Chicago and had gone on a picnic with one of the wealthiest summer guests. Andrew needed to learn more about the fellow.

After hitching up his team to the sickle bar mower, Andrew drove out to the hayfield. He loved the sound of the cutting teeth biting into the stalks and watching the swath of hay fall into a ribbon. Haying was hot and dusty work but seeing the growing heap of dried grass filling the barn loft gave him contentment and satisfaction. His animals would eat well this winter. Memories of Ginny riding on the load of hay swept over Andrew. He must erase those feelings. But instead, he felt the pressure of her fingers linked with his and reached for the lucky stone in his pocket.

Andrew called to his team as they entered the barnyard. Sweat slicked the horses' chests and legs. After leading them to a hitching post, Andrew drew off the harness, and brushed down the horses. He praised their hard work, checked the water level in the stock tank and released his team into the paddock. They munched oats before ambling out to the pasture to graze. He hung up the tack and out of the corner of his eye, spied Ginny strolling up the lane, swinging her milk bucket.

Because his mother had popped over to visit with Mrs. McVea, Andrew had his excuse. Ginny paused when he strode out to her. Was she so hurt from his last words that she would turn her back on him? She inched toward the milk house, and he met her at the door. Ginny's cream-colored shirtwaist highlighted the rose in her cheeks, and the waistband of her skirt emphasized her narrow curves. A small purple ribbon fluttered by her high collar. Confusion filled her upturned face.

"My mother is off visiting. She probably forgot what evening it was." Andrew had encouraged his mother to step out by not reminding her of what day it was.

"I see. How have you been?" Ginny cocked her head. "How are the peaches?"

Bereft. Heartsick. Lonely. Overwhelmed with the loss of you, Andrew wanted to say. "A new moth has invaded the peach orchard causing more damages."

Ginny frowned. "What sort of damages? What can you do?"

"Come." Andrew knew he shouldn't, but Elizabeth had not shown any interest in the new pest. He led Ginny to an infected tree where leaves drooped on the ends of several branches. "A moth lays her eggs in the tips of the branches and kills them. So, I've been pruning off the dying wood."

"I'm so sorry. I love how they look like green mustaches." Ginny's finger caressed a few of the glossy leaves. "Has the moth harmed the crop?"

"It has weakened the trees and they probably won't have as many blossoms next spring. But the storm took at least a third of the crop." Andrew wished he were the cluster of leaves sliding through her fingers.

"All that work." Ginny sighed. "I'm sorry. I hope you earn some profits."

"I hope so, too. Mother's even more adamant about selling the sheep pasture."

Ginny reached out her hand and then drew back. "Is there some other way of earning money?"

"I've been splitting wood and selling it in Shorewood." Andrew yearned for Ginny to complete her motion and touch his arm.

"We're almost out of wood. Could you drop off a load, please?"

"I would be glad to." Andrew started walking to the milk house. "So, what have you been doing?" He clenched his jaw, hoping Ginny wouldn't mention a particular gentleman. Did she know about Elizabeth and how she had rejected him?

"Sketching. Our chef is a student at the summer art school and gave me a sketch book. I had forgotten how much I enjoyed drawing." Ginny looked out at the Lake. "I wish I were as talented as some of the summer students who paint. How I would love to capture this image."

"Maybe you could take lessons." Andrew lifted a tall can and poured milk into Ginny's bucket.

"First I need to practice drawing." Ginny handed him her payment. "Thank you, it was nice to chat." She stared at her feet.

"Yes, it was." Andrew pocketed the change. "I'll bring round the wood tomorrow."

"Good night." Ginny ambled away.

Leaning against the door jam, Andrew stared at Ginny's hair blazing copper in the sunset, like when he had first spied her on the boat. In June, he had considered her a spoiled city girl, but over the summer she had proved herself a responsible woman who was willing to take risks and learn new skills. How skilled was she at kissing? Did her lips yearn for his? Would she wrap her arms around him so he could feel her smooth flesh? Andrew shook his head. He needed a dip in the Lake to dose the desire flooding him.

Chapter Twelve

In the gray dawn, Ginny crumpled newspaper, stuffed it into the fire box along with pine needles, and several sticks of kindling....she needed to split some more of it...and struck a match. She yawned, checked the small blaze, and added a few chunks of wood. What had been a daunting task had become part of her normal morning routine, one that she would miss when they returned to Chicago. Ginny slammed the door to the firebox. Perhaps if she ran off to Grand Rapids, she could hide from William until he gave up on her. Why was he so determined to marry her? Knowing William, he would hire a Pinkerton agent to sniff her out. The annoying fellow hovered over her like the red-tailed hawk circling Andrew's hay field, watching for a rabbit to dart across the mowed grass.

Standing at the sink, Ginny pumped water into a white china pitcher. How wonderful to talk to Andrew last night, to hear about his problems and determination to keep the pasture. To lose it would wound his love of beauty and the joy of watching the Lake throughout the day. But why had he been home instead of his mother? Had Andrew planned the meeting, or had it been by chance? His expression had revealed how his feelings for her lingered. Why did he refuse to acknowledge them? The rattle of a wagon rippled into the cottage. Ginny added water to the oatmeal and set the pot on the stove.

With his arms filled with wood, Andrew marched down the steps, and stacked it in the usual spot. Ginny closed the screen door softly. How she longed to feel his arms around her. To have a chance to kiss him until Andrew abandoned his silly ideas about her being like Nancy. Instead of William's unwanted poaching, she yearned for Andrew's caresses floating over her body as he taught her what lovemaking should feel like between a husband and a wife.

"Good morning." Ginny followed Andrew to the wagon and picked up several split logs.

"Good morning. You should let me haul the wood. It will dirty your pretty outfit."

"That's what aprons are for." Ginny added one more log and walked behind Andrew, reveling in his broad shoulders.

"I suppose so. What are your plans for the day?" Andrew ducked beneath a hemlock branch.

"Another boring ballgown fitting and then I plan to stay and sketch with the students." Ginny placed her logs on the stack. Andrew's jaw tightened at the mention of a ballgown. Was he jealous how other men would see her in it? How could she impress upon him that she would prefer to wear it for him instead of William?

"I'm glad you'll go sketching." Andrew placed his last chunks on the stack. "Do you think you'll want more wood next week?"

"Yes, please." Ginny wanted more of Andrew and envied the logs his hands had touched. "Mother is planning another dinner party so there will be extra baking and cooking."

"I'll bring it next Friday." Andrew nodded and strode up the path to his wagon.

Ginny returned to the kitchen, spooned black raspberries into fruit bowls and set the table for breakfast. Her father stood on the side porch staring out at the Lake. Maybe her father should have taken up painting or perhaps she should buy him one of those vest pocket Kodiak cameras and he could take photos of the lakeshore. She walked over to him.

"The Lake is always beautiful, isn't it?" If Ginny had been a child, she would have slid her hand into his, but the current tensions crackled between them.

"Yes, the view is fresh every morning." He squeezed her shoulder and looked down at the purple ribbon. "Must you wear that at breakfast, it upsets your mother so."

"I'll wait until later." Ginny unpinned the ribbon and slipped it into her apron pocket. "But I do believe in a woman's right to vote."

"I know. But be careful, daughter." Worry lines crinkled his forehead.

"That William won't want me?" Ginny hoped her views might discourage him.

"Or any other man. You may snub the society you were born into, but it's the only life you were prepared for."

Ginny wanted to point out how she had picked strawberries and helped spray an orchard, but thoughts of Nancy's suicide silenced her. Visiting the farm had taught her how demanding the labors could be and the perils lurking in a summer storm or a new insect invasion. But she was not Nancy and could learn to navigate such a life.

"Why is William so insistent about marrying me?" Ginny watched her father's face.

"He needs my money."

"I thought his family was wealthier than ours." Ginny frowned.

"At times they are. William tends to take risks in buying real estate and stocks, and currently he is deeply in debt. No one will lend him money. I try to save as much of my income as I can, which is why he is eyeing my bank account and especially your dowry."

"Papa! I'm not a piece of land to be bartered away." If her father had so much wealth, then she should marry

Andrew and her dowry could pay for the sheep pasture. Should she mention Andrew's debt?

Her father held up a hand. "Please listen to my thoughts. When I gain those shares of stocks, I will have as much control over William's company as he does. With the advice of my lawyers, I will straighten out the finances, pay off the debts, and ensure that the company makes a profit. I plan to arrange it so you will have a trust fund to supply you with spending money. Marriage is so much more than love, Ginny, and you need to consider how you can use your beauty and prestige for Chicago. Marrying into William's family will allow you to head charities and help those in need."

"But I would rather volunteer at the Settlement house and not just give money."

"I know, but if you asked the women running those institutions, they would rejoice if given a check. After you marry, I plan to annually donate a large sum to the place and other charities like it."

Turning away, Ginny bit her lower lip. She didn't want prestige or the power to influence Chicago, but she would appreciate how the yearly donation would help the Settlement House. Still, Ginny wished her father would invest his money in Andrew's farm and not William's failing company. Why couldn't her father see that William might squander his assets, again? She doubted if she could keep William's lecherous hands off her funds. After all, he always got what he wanted.

When the dressmaker's door closed, Ginny turned toward the art school. "I'll return home later this afternoon."

"If I allow this foolishness, you promise to attend the concert with William?" Her mother placed a hand on Ginny's arm.

"As long as we are chaperoned, yes." Ginny slipped out of her mother's grasp and strode to the hotel. Her purple ribbon fluttered in the breeze off the Kalamazoo River. Closing her eyes, she inhaled willing the tension to flow out of her. She may never be a good artist, but she would enjoy the time with the students.

"Ginny! Welcome." Anne waved her paint brush and a few droplets of yellow splattered her smock. "Come sit by me."

The other students added their greetings and returned to their paintings. Ginny slid into the offered wooden chair and opened her book. Anne peeked over her shoulder.

"Francis said you had a delicate touch and liked to focus on the whimsical side of your subjects."

"Sometimes it seems life is so serious; we need something light-hearted to perk us up." Ginny began to draw a duck floating on the river.

"I agree. That's why I love coming here. Leaving behind the tenements of Chicago, the noise of delivery wagons, and the stench of factory smoke. I keep hoping I can find a way to stay and live in Saugatuck."

"Me, too. I'd rather live here." Ginny flipped a page and sketched a man fishing from the boardwalk.

"Aren't you from a wealthy family? Francis said one of those Shorewood fellows wants to marry you."

"Yes, and what's worse is that my parents want me to marry him." Ginny pressed her lips into a thin line.

"Well, better to be rich than living in a tenement house." Anne dabbed her brush on her portrayal of a ship sailing into Saugatuck Harbor. "Is he a good kisser?"

Ginny blanched remembering William's lips smashed against her. Her hand shook and she dropped her pencil. William's rocking motion roiled her stomach and bile slicked her tongue. How could she endure a future with a man who had no respect for her? Every time he touched her Ginny would remember that vile moment. As his legal wife, she would have to submit to his advances and satisfy his lusts.

"One of those guys." Anne gazed out at the river. "Want to talk about it? I've met up with a couple of those types."

Could she trust Anne? She longed to confide in someone. To have a female friend to share her thoughts and questions. Ginny exhaled. "Yes, but could we go somewhere else?"

"Let me clean up and we'll head to my room." Anne rinsed her brushes and gathered her supplies.

Ginny followed Anne up to the second story of the hotel, down a hall, and into a small room with white-washed walls. Two narrow beds, a desk, two chairs and a washstand completed the furnishings along with a small wardrobe. Sketchbooks, stacks of watercolor paper, and dozens of drawings and paintings decorated the walls along with an oval mirror in an oak frame.

"Take a chair or sit on the bed if you prefer. Margaret is my roommate." Flinging aside her boots, Anne flopped down on her cot and stretched her arms over her head. "So, what happened?" She rolled onto her side and gazed into Ginny's face.

Staring at her hands, Ginny described the sailboat outing and her father's determination to marry her to William. At the end, she mentioned Andrew and how his wife's suicide had altered their growing relationship.

"So, you despise William and what he stands for and are in love with Andrew and his farm." Anne twirled a lock of her brown hair. "And you think he might still like you."

"Yes. I am grateful for all my parents have given me and want to make them happy, but it's 1915. Women don't have to accept what society dictates."

"Yes and no. In your social circle, you must follow those rules. But in more progressive situations, women are working as clerks in law firms, teaching at universities, and here in Saugatuck, women run shops like the dressmaker. What do you think about children?"

"Well, after I marry having children will be rewarding, especially if they were Andrew's and they could grow up on a farm."

"I was wondering if you might like to teach. The Douglas School has advertised for a teacher for the lower grades. You graduated from high school, correct?"

"Actually, from a ladies seminary that emphasized learning French over Algebra." Ginny scanned the drawings pinned to the wall. A couple of them were of nude women, and one of them looked like Anne. She fiddled with her soggy handkerchief. Had her friend posed for it?

"You could tutor young women after classes and on Saturdays. I bet there are mothers who would love to have their daughters learn French." Anne leaned over and ruffled through a stack of papers and pulled out a form. "I was thinking of applying but instead interviewed for a job here at the hotel. Spending all day with children would sap my creativity. Why don't you fill out the application, and I'll mail it."

"So, my parents won't find out about it? Thank you." Ginny accepted a fountain pen and wrote her name on the first line. What would her parents do if she were given the job? They would object and she would have to find a place to live.

"Yes. Have them send their response in care of my name to General Delivery at the Saugatuck Post Office. If you want, you could room with me. Margaret will be returning to Chicago in September. I need a little rest. Tonight, the manager is having me work in the dining room to see if I am qualified for the job." Anne closed her eyes.

Ginny filled in the blanks pausing at the ones asking for references. The only local people she knew were Andrew and his mother. Would they speak for her? The President of the Lakeshore Chapel knew her, but if she wrote in his name, he would talk to her parents. Wiping the pen nib, Ginny wrote in Andrew and Mrs. McBride's names and the other requested information.

Anne yawned. "Finished? Good. I hope we can enjoy the winter together."

"Thank you. I appreciate your help." Ginny nodded at the sketches. "Is that one of you?"

Anne winked. "It certainly is. I won't disrobe for my fellow students, but there's an artist in Chicago who hires me as a model. Hopefully at the end of the summer, he will visit Saugatuck. Margaret will have to sleep somewhere else that week." Anne laughed as red traveled around Ginny's neck. "You are so naïve. When you love someone, you long to satisfy him and encourage him to fulfill your desires."

"I hope I feel that way someday." Ginny swallowed remembering how Andrew had kindled longings inside her. "What's it like to model for him?" That was one job she would not pursue.

"I find it freeing and tend to float out of my body and view it as a piece of sculpture. The room is warm, and the student artists are focused on their work. I'm sure some of the men have other thoughts. Staying still is hard, but I've learned to dream about Lake Michigan or other peaceful scenes. And the pay is terrific."

"I see. Do you wear bloomers back in Chicago?" Ginny eyed the pairs hanging in the half-opened wardrobe.

"When I attend classes at the Institute, yes, but when walking around town I don a skirt."

"Might I please try on one of your pairs?" Ginny tucked her balled-up hanky into her skirt pocket. She might not have another chance.

"Certainly. Brown? Navy blue?" Anne pointed to the pairs.

"The brown ones, please." Ginny slipped out of her skirt and petticoats and drew on the bloomers.

"Oh my, your derriere fills them out perfectly. William would want to pinch it."

"I was afraid of that." Ginny stood on her toes so she could view her reflection in the mirror. What would Andrew think if he could see her? Bloomers would be more practical for a farm wife. They showed off her slender ankles, too.

Anne collapsed onto her bed laughing. "Your face says so much. Yes, Andrew would relish the sight of you."

Ginny stared at the mirror. Was she bold enough to wear bloomers? "Did you buy them here?"

"Yes, the little shop at the end of Butler Street has a few pair hidden under the counter. Tell Mrs. Connelly that Annie sent you."

"Thank you. What are you doing Sunday afternoon?" Ginny hung up the bloomers and pulled on her skirt.

"Nothing planned yet. What did you have in mind?"

***

"You need to attend the band concert where you might run into a girl you know." Andrew's mother buttered her toast. "After all, it's Sunday and we could walk over to Saugatuck after the church service."

"Maybe I don't want to go and would prefer to rest or to walk on the beach." Andrew sipped his tea. He didn't need his former school friends to tease him about a rejected courtship. Attending the concert with his mother would make him feel like a ten-year-old.

"If you promise to go, then I'll come home. You need to get out and meet women or you'll never find a wife." His mother swept a few breadcrumbs into the palm of her hand. "Forget about Ginny."

Her hair still glowed in the sunsets. Her eyes shimmered like the glossy peach leaves. When he stood on the beach, her fingers twined with his. But the Shorewood gossips whispered about a certain fellow named William and how they expected him to announce his engagement to Ginny. When delivering wood, Andrew had spied the man her father had chosen for his daughter and had witnessed the arrogance in his eyes. Should Andrew interfere, or had Ginny accepted her future in society? Hadn't he encouraged her to return to that world? He ran a hand down the left side of his face.

"I'll go, but alone." Andrew shoved in his chair. He wouldn't stay long and would clear his mind by walking home along the beach. By sunset, he would stand once more in his orchard removing dead leaves.

After the church service, Andrew strolled toward the lilting phrase of a Sousa waltz performed by a concert brass band. In a small park, the musicians in black suits played inside a white gazebo with lattice trimming the railing. Around the gazebo sat couples and families on wooden folding chairs or blankets. The women wore white lawn dresses and wide brimmed hats trimmed with feathers and silk flowers. While the men sported linen suits or beige trousers and white shirts. The sunlight sparkled on the Kalamazoo River where couples rowed boats or paddled canoes. A few serving staff from the Butler Hotel clustered by a stand of maples where three artists with their easels painted the scene.

Ginny's laughter floated through the crowd and Andrew winced. He had assumed she would attend this event and sit next to her Shorewood beau. But instead of chatting with what's-his-name, Ginny leaned toward a woman dressed in a white shirtwaist and gray bloomers. The two of them laughed again and her beau frowned. He tried to interrupt their conversation, but Ginny ignored him. She had never treated Andrew in that manner, but then other than his mother, they were seldom with another person. Ginny glanced at him and spoke to her female friend who nodded her head.

"Andrew!" Ginny called. "Come join us!"

Was Ginny crazy? But he didn't want her to shout his name again. Thrusting his hands in his pockets, Andrew walked around the perimeter of the gathering, found a narrow opening between chairs, and aimed for Ginny. She wore a pale blue lawn dress with three-quarter-length sleeves and a lacy bodice where a purple ribbon fluttered. Smiling up at him, Ginny's face radiated tenderness and Andrew wanted to run his fingertips along her cheek.

"Good afternoon, Andrew. Please meet William and my friend and chaperone, Anne from the art school."

Anne patted an empty wooden chair next to her. "Please sit with us, unless you were planning to join another party?"

"Thank you." Andrew eased onto the edge of the seat as William glared at Ginny and Anne. What was Ginny up to? Surely, she understood how she had created a sticky situation for him? Or had she planned this? As if the four of them were old friends, they sat in the middle of the small crowd. How odd Ginny had chosen a young lady as her chaperone. Granted, most of the time an older matron oversaw a courting couple and not an artist wearing bloomers and a purple ribbon. Had Ginny heard about Elizabeth and thought he should become friends with the artist? William's expression showed his fury.

"Aren't you the fellow who delivers the firewood?" William glanced at Andrew. "You mow lawns, too?"

Andrew's neck reddened. Is that how Ginny portrayed him? Not that he would look down at a groundskeeper, but he preferred to be recognized as a farmer. The conductor waved his baton, and a lone trombone player began a march.

"Oh, William, really." Anne shook her head. "Andrew is a fruit farmer. He grew those luscious strawberries you ate this spring and soon he will pick the most beautiful peaches on the lakeshore. Ginny raves about his orchards, the cream from his cows, and the time when she rode on a load of hay. You should listen better." Anne leaned back in her chair as the trumpets joined into the tune.

Pulling out his handkerchief, Andrew wiped his forehead. Ginny had described him in those glowing terms. And she hadn't criticized Anne for chastising William. How serious was she about this courtship? Andrew relished the anger stiffening William's jaw and how it snapped in his dark eyes. Other than the man's mother, probably no woman had rebuked William, and certainly not in public.

"When the concert ends, we are going to have sodas, would you like to join us?" Ginny asked.

"I thought we would go on a buggy ride before I dropped you off." William touched Ginny's arm.

"You promised sodas for Anne and me, and I'm sure Andrew likes ice cream, too."

William scowled. "I guess I did. Afterwards we *will* have that ride."

Ginny's face paled and she fiddled with her purple ribbon. Andrew rubbed his palms down his thighs. Most courting women wanted to be alone with their young men and encouraged buggy rides down narrow wayside roads where they could linger and kiss. One evening, he and

Nancy had taken his wagon to Goshorn Lake and hidden it behind a cluster of hemlock trees. Spreading several quilts over the wagon bed, he had lifted her skirt while she slid her hand down his trousers. Andrew longed to question Ginny about her relationship with William.

When the march ended, the audience applauded, and the conductor bowed twice before extending a hand toward the musicians. The men stood, nodded, and began packing their instruments. People gathered up blankets and folded chairs. The serving staff from the Butler placed the remaining chairs in a wagon and carried them back to the hotel. Anne leaned over and whispered something into Ginny's ear. The two girls laughed. William slid his arm through Ginny's, so Andrew offered his to Anne.

"Thank you. My you have strong hands and I've heard about your shoulder muscles." Anne glanced up at Andrew. "I'd like to see you in a swimsuit. Ginny said you were stunning."

"Thank you." Andrew blushed. No woman had spoken so boldly to him. His mother wouldn't approve of Anne, but his instincts hinted that the girl's words were aimed at William who hastened his pace.

At the drug store, Andrew held opened the door as the others walked inside. The sugary fragrance of chocolate and butterscotch swirled around the counter where mothers and fathers ordered ice cream for their children. Other courting couples held hands as they waited and chatted. But Ginny withdrew her elbow and stepped away from William. What would she do if Andrew slipped his fingers through hers? Rolling his hat through his hands, Andrew focused on the white board displaying the different options for sodas and sundaes.

***

"I'll have a chocolate soda with chocolate ice cream." Ginny glanced at William's flushed face. "Thank you for treating us." She squeezed her lips together to suppress a laugh. Anne's suggestion would infuriate William further and would hopefully initiate the end of their courtship.

"Me, too," Anne said. "What about you, Andrew?"

"I'll have a root beer float," he said.

William rattled off the orders including his vanilla soda and when other customers vacated their spots at the red counter, the four of them perched on the stools. Ginny scanned the narrow room with a few round tables surrounded by four chairs. Long spoons clinked against the tulip shaped soda glasses and other folks dug into their hot fudge sundaes. Everyone's expression displayed pleasure and happiness, except for William who shifted his weight on the stool and drummed his fingers. Of course, Anne's scheme might make William fight harder to keep her as his girlfriend. She shuddered. Then she and Anne would have to concoct another plan.

Ginny peeked at Andrew chatting with Anne. Her friend understood how to flirt in a jolly manner and not tempt Andrew with improper thoughts. Ginny wished her acquaintances in Chicago had been schooled in becoming friends with men. Andrew appeared relaxed but the small worry lines by his eyes told her that he would prefer to work in his orchard. The server brought their ice cream and the talking ceased.

Through a straw, Ginny sipped the sweet chocolate soda water relishing the tingle in her nose. From the way William attacked his treat, he should chomp on the glass and consume the spoon. He didn't bother to talk to her but glared at Andrew and Anne. Her father might have tried to explain his reasons for marrying William, but his logic had not convinced Ginny.

"Aren't you done yet?" William shoved his empty glass at the server.

"No." Ginny slid a tiny bite of ice cream into her mouth and closed her eyes. She loved how the soda water dimpled the ice cream. Little by little, she ate the treat while matching her motions to Anne's. With his hands in his pockets, William got up and wandered the drug store aisles. When Anne set her spoon in her glass and stood, Ginny followed suit. Andrew placed his hat on his head and escorted Anne out the door and William grabbed Ginny's arm.

"Thank you for the soda," Anne said to William.

"You're welcome." William pushed Ginny towards their rented buggy.

"Why don't you offer Andrew a ride home?" Anne raised her voice. "You're going his way."

William whirled around. "And why don't you mind your own business? Go draw or something."

"A proper chaperone must consider her charge's reputation. Andrew is well known in the area and could serve as a companion for the homeward trip."

"A lovely idea." Ginny smiled at Andrew's startled face. "And I'm sure you are weary after working so hard this past week. A ride would give you more rest." She hoped the look in her eyes conveyed her need for him to save her from being alone with William.

"Thank you. I would appreciate it, then I'd be home in time to milk."

Ginny enjoyed William's red face and half-closed eyes as they darted between Anne and herself. He exhaled and swept a hand toward the buggy. "Hop in."

Andrew nodded and offered his hand to Ginny so that she could slide onto the buggy seat. William climbed up, and Andrew followed. William flicked the buggy whip and the mare trotted off. With a tug on the reins, William steered the buggy toward the ferry. Once aboard, Ginny leaned against the railing, gazing up at the rows of small cumulus clouds floating from the west. A tugboat's whistle blew, and a duck bobbed as the ferry's wake reached it. She was a duck floating in William's anger. When the ferry reached the other riverbank, William shook the reins, the horse trotted, and they rolled towards Campbell Street. Now and then, the buggy rocked as a wheel sank into a rut. Soon, one of the wheels began to rattle and the buggy swayed as the wheel twisted from side to side. Ginny clutched the seat, and William swore. Andrew snatched the reins.

"Whoa!" he called to the mare and pulled the buggy to the side of the road. "Let me take a look." He jumped down and squatted by the offending wheel as William peered over the edge.

"See this tiny space. Looks like there was a shim to tighten the wheel to the axel and the shim fell out." Andrew snapped a twig and stuck it into the gap.

"I will complain to the livery. They were supposed to inspect the buggy before leasing it." William slapped a hand against the buggy seat.

"I'm sure it was a mistake," Ginny said.

"Perhaps we should slow down. Hitting the bumps might have knocked out the shim. You are used to driving on smoother roads in Chicago," Andrew said. "I can drive if you want."

"Absolutely not." William shook the reins. They rode in silence until reaching the entrance to the path leading to Ginny's cottage and the turn off to Shorewood. William pulled on the reins. Andrew leapt down.

"Since you're headed into Shorewood, I'll see Miss Ginny to her door." Andrew held out his hand to Ginny who accepted it.

William muttered and glared at Andrew. "I will see you at the dinner party tomorrow night, Virginia."

Ginny and Andrew ambled down the path and paused beneath a young hemlock.

"Thank you. I hope we didn't impose upon your afternoon. Anne can be quite bold." Ginny gazed out at the Lake. "I told my parents that I would not be alone with William and must have a chaperone. Anne volunteered. She probably seems odd to you."

"A little, but I'm used to various types of summer visitors. She has creative ways to implement her tricks."

Andrew laughed. "Thank you for including me." He strolled toward his farm.

Ginny ran to the beach and stared out at the waves. She loved the tenderness in Andrew's eyes, and how his smile tugged at the corners of his mouth. She yearned to feel his lips on hers, erasing the miserable memories of William. If Anne's ideas worked that moment would soon happen. Squatting down, she picked up a lucky stone and made a wish.

Chapter Thirteen

Do you know anything about this? Andrew's mother held out a letter. Outside the kitchen a flock of crows cawed, and their rooster crowed. She stirred cream and sugar in her tea and glanced up at Andrew.

"No, but I haven't talked much with Ginny. She's a hard worker and would make a fine teacher." Andrew slipped the letter back into the envelope. "We should write our references today."

His mother frowned. "Are you sure about this? I wonder what Ginny's parents think of her teaching. Isn't she engaged to that rich man?"

"Not yet." Andrew balled his napkin and tossed it onto the table. Picking up his breakfast dishes, he set them by the sink, and headed to the parlor to write his letter.

From a corner in the barn, Andrew picked up empty peach baskets and loaded them onto his wagon. He had surmised the meaning behind Ginny's comment about not wanting to be alone with William, and he longed to land a fist against the man's jaw. How dare William grab what wasn't offered. Seeking a teaching job would ensure that Ginny could stay on the lakeshore and avoid marrying William. But what if she was so repelled by the man that Ginny no longer wanted to marry anyone including himself? Andrew gazed out at the shifting blues on Lake Michigan. Her safety and happiness depended upon getting the teaching job.

Several hours later, Andrew gulped switchel from a jug and wiped his mouth with his shirt sleeve. Every morning for the next two weeks, he would pick the ripe peaches and sell them hoping to earn enough profit to pay the hardware bill and the bank. Today, he would deliver orders to Shorewood and to Ginny. He clucked to his team, and they stepped onto the road. At Ginny's cottage, he tied the horses to a tree and picked up two small baskets of peaches. Laughter rippled from the side porch where Ginny snapped beans and Francis critiqued her sketchbook.

"This one of the cats is wonderful." Francis pointed to how Ginny had shaded the creature. "You have a knack for capturing the animals' personalities."

"Thank you." Ginny glanced up. "Andrew. How lovely. My favorite fruit." She opened the screen door for him.

"Mmmm, peach cobbler tonight." Francis picked up a blushing orb and sniffed it. "They are perfect."

"Thank you. And thank you for your help in the orchard." Should he mention the reference he had written. Andrew wondered if Francis knew of Ginny's secret. He couldn't take the chance of anyone speaking of it to Ginny's parents. "I'll bring by more in a few days."

"Yes, please." Francis carried the baskets into the kitchen.

"I'll walk you to your wagon." Ginny looked at where her parents sat on the side porch visiting with a couple from Shorewood. They ambled up the path and paused by the team.

"We wrote the references." Andrew untied the reins from the tree. "Mother will mail them today."

"Thank you, thank you." Ginny leaned against the tree. "I'll let you know what happens."

Andrew yearned to hug her and reassure her how he would help Ginny in any way that he could, but instead he climbed up onto the wagon. He tipped his hat and drove into Shorewood.

The two-story clapboard cottages with gables and wide wrap around porches were larger than his farmhouse. Why these folks invested in such luxury baffled Andrew because back in Chicago their houses rivaled these cottages. One-by-one, he dropped off baskets at back doors and glimpse wallpapered walls, heavy velvet settees, and dark woodwork. Even in the kitchens, wooden wainscoting ran around the bottom of the walls. Finally, Andrew reached the house where Elizabeth cooked. When he had unloaded firewood, she had waved at him but hadn't come out to talk.

Picking up a basket, he walked down a winding brick path edged with hollyhocks. He rapped on the kitchen door and spied a couple kissing. Elizabeth gasped and shoved away the young handy man who worked for the family. Andrew grimaced. His heart had sensed this truth, but it hurt that Elizabeth had refused him. Setting the basket on the kitchen floor, Andrew looked into her eyes.

"You can add it to your bill for the firewood." Andrew strode to his wagon and rode home. He unhitched the team, brushed the horses, and sent them into the paddock where they drank for a good minute. Pulling out his handkerchief, he wiped his face and noticed his lucky stone had fallen onto the ground. He made a wish and stuffed it back into his pocket.

***

"This came for you." Anne dropped a letter on top of Ginny's sketch book. "What does it say?" Anne set up her easel as the other students also prepared to paint the park with the gazebo.

"The head of the schoolboard wants to interview me." Ginny showed her the letter. "On Wednesday at eleven in the Methodist Church. I'm supposed to have lunch with William's mother at that time."

"Well, let's think." Anne swished her brush in a tin bucket of water. "You can't pretend to be ill because then you would have to stay in bed."

"But I could come to sketching and lose track of the time." Ginny drew the lattice work on the gazebo. "Usually, the actual meal doesn't begin until noon, so perhaps I could arrive a little late."

"Hopefully, the interview won't last more than thirty minutes." Anne dabbed her brush into a patch of green paint. "But what if it does?"

"Then my mother will spend the rest of the day scolding me until I can escape to the sandbar." From her memory, Ginny drew the musicians seated in the gazebo. She had dreaded going to the concert until Anne offered to chaperone. How did her friend conceive such tricks such as inviting Andrew to ride with them in the buggy? Ginny wished she were aa clever as Anne.

On Wednesday morning, Ginny left her purple pin on her dresser and donned a white shirtwaist with a pleated front and a navy-blue skirt. Turning around, she examined her profile in the mirror. Her outfit shouldn't offend the schoolboard chairman and should convince him how she was no different from the local young women. She pinned on a straw hat decorated with pink silk roses. Picking up her sketchbook, Ginny headed to the back door, but her mother blocked her path.

"Where are you going? That outfit is not proper attire for the luncheon. And I must arrange your hair in a more attractive style. Your appearance must please William."

"I'm meeting my friends to sketch for an hour or so. I'll try and be back on time." Ginny stepped around her mother.

"*You'll try?*" Her mother sputtered.

"Yes." Ginny dashed out the door, up the path and hastened to the ferry.

"Good luck," Anne said when the church bells chimed ten-thirty. "You look like a proper schoolmarm. It's a pity that you don't wear glasses."

Ginny smiled and fingered the lucky stone in her pocket. "You should have been an actress." For Anne, life was about drama, but instead of a stage, Anne chose to paint her stories.

"And you are headed for an audition." Anne laughed.

At the Methodist Church, Ginny opened the door and spotted two men in suits walking down a hall, so she followed them. One turned and spied her while the other entered a room.

"Miss Madden?" I'm Michael Larson the head of the school board." He extended his hand.

"Pleased to meet you, sir, and thank you for inviting me for this interview." Ginny and Anne had practiced this moment so her brain wouldn't abandon her.

"We're meeting in here close to the pastor's office and will leave the door open. This is Mr. Henry Butler."

Mr. Butler nodded and shook Ginny's hand. "Nice to meet you." His eyes swept over her.

"Thank you for this interview, sir." Beneath her long skirt her knees shook. Ginny knew how to interact with the older wealthy men her father invited to their home, but this duo had the hands of working men. Think of them as Andrew's father, she told herself, or an older version of Andrew. But her future sat on their swaying scales.

"Please take a seat," Mr. Larson said. The men sat down at a small table and spread before them her application. "We were impressed with your education but have a few questions."

Ginny folded her hands in her lap and wished she could hide them beneath an apron. "I will gladly answer them, sir."

"Your only prior teaching experience was to tutor the younger students at the seminary you attended?" Mr. Butler asked.

"Yes, sir. Throughout my last four years, I helped the first and second graders with their reading and arithmetic." Ginny hadn't thought to ask the headmistress for a reference, would this oversight work against her?

"Good. You also speak French?" Mr. Larson asked.

"Tolerably well, sir. At graduation, I earned an award." Wearing a white dress with a blue sash, Ginny had accepted a crystal vase filled with a bouquet of pink roses as her prize. Her mother had wept over her daughter's accomplishments and crowed about how they would help her marry well. What would her mother think now if speaking French would help her claim this position?

"Excellent, congratulations. Any other skills you didn't share?" Mr. Butler asked.

"I could teach sketching to those interested in art and also offer ball room dancing lessons, sir." Ginny had mentioned those ideas to Anne who had insisted they might be the keys to the job.

"Wonderful additions." Mr. Larson glanced at his partner. "Yet, our main question is why a young woman of your breeding would want to teach school in Douglas?" Both men stared at her.

Ginny gazed out the window for a few seconds before turning back to the men who could unlock the gate to the path she yearned to explore. "I have made friends here and enjoy the quieter life a small town provides. I found tutoring children rewarding and thought I would make a good teacher, sir. Most of all, I love Lake Michigan and I'm sure you hold similar feelings for this special place."

"Yes." Mr. Larson nodded his head. "But our winters are long, cold and snowy with few entertainments."

"I considered that, but Chicago's temperatures can be even colder, sir. And a person can create their own entertainment with snow shoeing outings or perhaps organizing a Chautauqua for the community's benefit." Thank goodness for Anne who had suggested that idea.

"Yes. That's true. Well, thank you for your time. We have two more candidates to interview and will let you know which person we choose." Mr. Larson rose and escorted Ginny to the main door. "Good-by, Miss Madden."

"Thank you, sir. May you have a good week." Ginny walked out into the sunshine where a young man waited. Might the schoolboard prefer a man who could better handle the boys? Ginny pushed away the thought as she dashed to the ferry.

After the luncheon, her mother waited until they had walked far enough away from William's cottage before snatching Ginny's wrist. "How dare you treat your future mother-in-law in such a rude manner. A half-an-hour late. That's what becomes of socializing with those artists."

Ginny pressed her lips into a thin line. No excuses would reduce her mother's anger. She wanted to point out how William hadn't asked her to marry him, so his mother couldn't claim any relationship to her. Instead, Ginny stared at the Lake and counted how many steps it took to reach their path and then to their cottage. She marched to her room, threw off her clothes, and drew on her swimming outfit.

Standing on the beach, she studied the pewter-colored, three-foot high waves rolling in from the northwest and smashing against the sandbar, but the water nearby appeared calmer. She would float down the lakeshore a bit and then walk home. All that mattered was to feel the arms of the Lake comforting her and washing away her mother's wrath. She dove into the water.

Ginny gasped as a current generated by the waves clutched her legs, wrapped itself around her body, and dragged her away from the shore. She screamed but the roar of the waves hitting the sand bar smothered her voice. She thrashed her arms, but the current tugged harder. Her heart pounded and fear snatched her breath as the sight of her cottage dwindled. Was she going to drown? What should she do?

Relax, her body whispered, save your strength, and think. Ginny tread water as her mind settled. Perhaps, she could fight the current by swimming along the shore while watching for someone she could call to. Arm over arm, she swam; little-by-little she angled toward the beach. Despite growing heavier and weary, Ginny kicked her legs. Her shoulders ached and began to quiver. How much longer could she resist?

***

Andrew threw down his towel and dove into the lake. Water sluiced off him as he rose and scooped up handfuls, splashing his neck and arms. Nothing eased the misery of peach fuzz like the sweetness of Lake Michigan. How did those Georgia farmers cool their body temperatures and scrub away the itching?

Scanning the shoreline, Andrew smiled at the children dashing in and out of where the waves broke upon the shore. Mothers and fathers stood by their offspring ready to nab any child who might tumble. A few older couples sat on quilts or folding wooden chairs enjoying the breeze and view. Farther out from shore someone swam. Andrew frowned. Did that person know how rip currents lurked when high waves broke upon the sandbar? The head rose and shouted.

Great heavens, it was Ginny. Andrew looked about and spied a thick board toss ashore after a recent storm. Grabbing it, he ran into the waves, thrust the board in front of him, and kicked his legs. Anger and fear fueled him. The lake he cherished would not swallow the woman he loved. He plowed through the rip current, and Ginny's frightened face materialized as he drew closer. Gauging the movement of the current, he angled toward her.

"Grab the board!" He pushed it forward. Ginny threw herself onto it and they began to sink. "No, Ginny! Hold onto it!"

Ginny eased off and clutched the edge, positioning herself about two feet from Andrew. He turned toward the shore and kicked once more, heaving them free from the rip current. Although her legs moved slowly Ginny swam, too.

"That's my girl!" Andrew shouted. "Moving will keep you warm. Almost there."

A small crowd had gathered at his towel and cheered them on. Andrew wished those folks would return to their own beaches so he and Ginny could be alone. When their feet hit the sand, he threw the board onto the beach and scooped up Ginny. The people clapped and praised Andrew as he walked up the dune.

"Thank you!" He called back. "I need to get her to my mother."

"I can walk. I think." She wrapped an arm around his waist and leaned against him.

"Let's get away from the crowd."

At the top of the path, they sank down and collapsed against the rail fence. Andrew inhaled as his heartbeat slowed and his muscles quivered. His mind pushed aside thoughts of what might have happened to them if the Lake had won the battle.

"Thank God you are alive. I'll take you home, soon, but what happened?" Andrew slid his fingers through hers.

***

Ginny squeezed Andrew's hand. She rested her head on his shoulder and breathed in his scent. Still shaking, she explained about the interview, the luncheon, her mother's anger, and how the current had snatched her. The sunshine massaged her weary legs and arms, and Andrew's expression soothed her heart.

"Andrew, I'm not Nancy. Please, can't we be friends again?" Ginny bit her lower lip. "If I get the job, it would be nice to see you now and then."

"No." Andrew looked across the pasture and shook his head. "No. I want to be more than friends." Leaning over, he cupped her chin in his palms and kissed her.

Ginny drank in the softness of Andrew's lips and the feel of his fingers on her chin. Heat rose in her belly and scorched the memories of William's assault. As Andrew's thumb caressed her cheek, she ran a hand down his arm cherishing the muscles that had saved her life. She threaded her fingers through his hair, and wrapped her arms around his neck.

"More please." She pressed her lips over his and her tongue slid into his mouth. A rush of fire erupted in her veins as Andrew's tongue met hers. The sun's warmth sweetened their kiss and Ginny longed to remain in Andrew's arms until the sunset. Now she could tell Anne how Andrew was a wonderful kisser.

"Ginny. While I would love to spread a blanket in the hay mow and continue." Andrew grasped her shoulders and scooted away from her. "I need to ask your father if I may court you before we regret anything. But first you must talk to William."

Although she ached with desire, Ginny slumped against the fence. She longed to join Andrew anywhere if he would resume kissing her. "You are right. I'll speak with William at the ball tomorrow." Blast it all, she had no use for the stupid ball but at least William couldn't throw too much of a fit in front of everyone.

"Good." Andrew kissed the tip of her nose. "Don't look at me like that. Remember I was a married man, and those same longings linger. I know what I would like to do with you." He nuzzled her neck and kissed her behind her ear.

"I can't wait to find out." Ginny took Andrew's hand as he helped her to her feet.

"You can borrow a shawl or something from my mother and I'll give you a ride home." Andrew slid an arm around her waist. "I'm sure you are tired."

"I am. Thank you." Ginny wrapped an arm around Andrew. Somehow, she would convince her parents that Andrew was the right husband for her.

Chapter Fourteen

In the gray light of early dawn, someone knocked on the side porch screen door and Ginny turned around. "Anne! Come on in."

"Good news." Anne handed Ginny the envelope. "It was in the mail last night, but I thought it would be better to come now. Open it! What a lovely cottage you have. Not as elaborate as those Shorewood places."

"Yes, I love our humble cottage. Wish me luck." Taking a knife, Ginny slit the envelope and pulled out the letter. She threw her arms around Anne. "I got the job! I'm staying! We can room together." While Anne read the letter, Ginny leaned against the table. "Now I have to figure out how to tell my parents. And William." Recalling Andrew's words, Ginny vowed to dismiss William tonight.

"And tell Andrew, his kisses can keep you warm this winter." Anne gave back the letter. "Too bad there's that ball, Mrs. Lewis, the woman organizing the local suffrage movement called for a rally tonight. It would be fun if you could come."

"I'd rather go to the rally than the ball, but so be it. Hopefully, there will be other events this fall." Ginny grinned. "I need one of those green and purple sashes. I can lend you a white dress."

"Hmm, could I please borrow one of your new frocks? A certain artist from Chicago will arrive tonight." Anne winked.

"I thought you took your clothes off for him." Ginny nudged Anne.

"Miss Madden! Such talk from a lady." Anne straightened her spine. "A dress, please."

"Just a minute. Keep an eye on the bacon." Ginny dashed to her room, grabbed the pink lawn, and rushed into the kitchen. "I can hear my parents. You had better leave." Folding the dress, she gave it to Anne. "I hope you charm him into marrying you."

"Only if he wants to set up a studio in Saugatuck." Anne blew Ginny a kiss.

"You're radiant." Her mother fluffed the black lace ruffle on Ginny's ballgown, so it brushed the tops of her breasts. "Being in love makes you glow."

Yes, knowing Andrew loved her brought rose to Ginny's cheeks and merriment to her eyes. What would it feel like to have Andrew unhook the back of this dress and slide down the bodice? Or would he first tease her by moving his lips along what the ruffle embellished? She blushed and her mother laughed.

"I knew William would be the one." She pulled Ginny from her room. "Mr. Madden, you must admire your daughter." Her mother turned Ginny around as if she were a figurine on top of a music box. "Have you ever seen anyone lovelier?"

"Only you. Ginny, you will stun every fellow in the room." He offered her his arm. "But first this gray-haired gentleman requests the honor of escorting you. After tonight, I may not have this chance until you walk done the aisle."

"Oh, Papa. Just a minute. I must fetch my shawl." Ginny stepped into her room and paused. She needed courage to face William. Picking up the purple ribbon, she pinned it beneath the black ruffle. A suffragist exemplified the courage for a woman to think for herself. She grabbed her lacy white Shetland shawl and returned to her father's side.

With her mother on her father's other arm, they strolled through Shorewood toward William's family's cottage. Lights illuminated every window and the rich scent of melting cheese and bar-b-que meatballs floated from the kitchen. Buggies were tied to hitching posts, and the horses stood switching their tails and dozing. The sweet melody of a waltz played by a cello, two violins and a viola greeted Ginny as she and her parents entered the cottage. A maid took her shawl and they stepped into a grand parlor.

The furniture had been removed, the Turkish carpets rolled up, and the floor polished until it reflected the dozens of candles in the Waterford chandelier and the glow of paraffin lamps. Cream-colored wallpaper with large bouquets of pink cabbage roses covered the walls and the dark wood trim around the windows glistened. In one corner, four male musicians in black suits played their instruments. A pocket door had been hidden inside a wall, enlarging the parlor, and allowing dancers to slide over to another room where tables offered a buffet. Other folks waltzed on the wrap around porch connected to the parlor. As soon as Ginny entered, William strode

to her side.

"Welcome Mr. and Mrs. Madden. Virginia, you are ravishing." William kissed her hand.

"Thank you." Ginny wanted to slap him. The glint in his eyes showed how William wanted to ravish her and she would not agree to a garden stroll. When and where should she speak to him? Perhaps on the porch?

"May I have this dance?" William slipped his hand onto her shoulder and propelled her to the dance floor. His other hand gripped her waist, and he pulled her closer. "Waltzes are so romantic, don't you think?" He whispered in her ear. "Seeing us together makes the other guests smile. Two old families uniting their children. Shorewood prefers those sorts of marriages. Shall we announce our engagement tonight?"

"I think not." Easing herself away from William, Ginny stiffened her back. How could she say anything while so many people watched them?"

"Ah, my beauty wants a separate party devoted to her and the announcement." William leaned over and kissed her behind the ear. "Then you shall have it my love and my dove."

Ginny had to stop the spread of misconceptions before people would assume they were engaged. Three older women sitting on a settee who had witnessed the kiss tittered. Her mother pointed at her and William and spoke to her friends. The next time William demanded her attentions, Ginny would suggest they dance on the porch where she could give her speech.

***

Andrew paced the barn. Ginny was at the ball dancing with William. Would the music and William's charms erase her affections for a common farmer? He gazed at the sun filling the west with rose and dusky blue as small clouds dimpled the sky. Tomorrow should be a sunny day. Lifting a handful of straw, Andrew let the stalks drop one-by-one.

Should he hitch up the wagon and drive to Shorewood and eavesdrop? He didn't want to be arrested for prowling around the fellow's cottage, but Ginny's remark of avoiding being alone with William pricked him. What if William dragged her away from the music and lights? Would anyone hear her scream?

"Andrew." His mother stood in the doorway of the barn. "You weren't invited."

"I know." He dropped the last of the straw. "But I feel as if she will need me."

"I baked molasses cookies, come in and have some." His mother nodded at the house.

"No, thank you." As if the sun sighed, bands of light radiated from its fiery center as it slipped below the horizon. A sliver from the straw shot pain through his thumb. Andrew dug it out and reached for the harness. His mother shook her head and departed.

Tugging on the reins, Andrew turned onto the private road leading into Shorewood. He had tossed several chunks of wood into the wagon as an excuse for driving onto the grounds. The phrases of a polka floated from

William's cottage. Andrew tied up his team to a small tree and leaned against his wagon. If he stayed here, he couldn't hear any conversations. *You came in case she screams,* his inner voice scolded him. So, he would wait and listen.

***

Taking her shoulder, William guided Ginny onto the porch and placed his hands on her waist. "How about we try this waltz hold." He drew her to his chest, leaned over, and kissed her lips.

"William. We are not alone." Ginny pushed him to a respectable distance. She had to stop his pawing hands that had slid down and squeezed her rear end. *Now, say everything now.*

"Well, we can be alone in the garden." William shoved her toward the screen door.

"No!" Ginny wrestled herself free as the other couples glanced at them. "No, no more dances. No more courting. No. No. No." Her voice rose higher and stronger. "I will not marry you. And I don't care what lies you tell people about me."

The music had ended, and the other dancers stared at William and Ginny. She glared up at William as the whispering rippled around them.

"Be careful, Virginia. You don't want to do this to yourself." William's eyes glinted. "I'll make sure that no other man will want you."

Ginny laughed and laughed. As if she cared about what these haughty men thought of her. Tears rolled down her cheeks and she collapsed into a chair as her mother and father rushed onto the porch. She wouldn't waste her time telling William about Andrew. He would soon learn of the man who had declared his love.

"She's hysterical, William. Don't listen to her." Her mother patted Ginny's cheek. "She's beside herself."

"Oh, no I'm not!" Ginny screamed out the words. "I finally am myself! And I refuse to be anyone else." She stood up. Her father grabbed her arm, but she removed his hand. "I'm leaving."

"You are out of your mind," her mother said. "We need to take you home. She needs rest."

"No." Ginny shoved open the screen door and ran down the brick path. Home was not where she needed to be.

***

As the waltz ended, Andrew ceased musing about holding Ginny in his arms and dancing. He cocked his head. That was Ginny's voice, but she didn't sound scared and threatened, she was angry. When she laughed, he chuckled. Perhaps she had slapped that arrogant William for stealing a kiss. Why were her parents involved in the argument? Footsteps slapped the path.

Ginny's hair blazed like embers in a fireplace and determination gleamed in her eyes. Andrew longed to embrace her, but Ginny's cross expression stilled his instincts. She gasped and stared at him.

"What are you doing here?" Ginny ran to him and slid her arms around his waist.

"I felt uneasy about William and thought I should wait here in case you needed help. But from what I overheard you controlled the situation." Andrew pressed her against him. She was safe and that was why he had come.

"Barely. Could you take me to Saugatuck, please? I would like to attend something."

"The rally? Certainly." Andrew offered his hand. "You are stunning in that gown."

He eyed the form fitting bodice and the curve of her hips revealed by the flow of the silk. The ruffle emphasized the swell of her breasts and sparked a fire in his veins. But the sound of her parents' and William's voices drew closer. Jumping onto the wagon seat, Andrew clucked to the horses, and they headed toward the ferry. A sliver of a moon lighted the road and lanterns glowed in the few farmhouses and cottages they passed. A screech owl whinnied as bats fluttered overhead. At the crest of a hill under the shelter of a cluster of hemlocks, Andrew pulled on the reins.

Ginny's fingertips stroked his cheek and lifted her face. "The school hired me. I'll stay on and room with Anne."

"Congratulations. I'm so thankful." He bent his head as she slipped her arms around his neck. Brushing her lips, his tongue drew halos over her mouth as his thumbs strolled down her ribs. He loved how she melted against him and he inhaled her violet perfume. Lowering his mouth, his lips crept over her collarbones and his pulse raced. Her mouth sought his and Andrew moaned.

"Thank you for this interlude, but the rally?" Ginny nuzzled his neck. "We could continue this later."

"Promise?" Andrew kissed her again. "To the rally." He released Ginny and picked up the reins. When they reached the landing, he leapt down, rang the bell, and stood by his team as the ferry chain rattled.

***

Wishing she had worn a white dress Ginny moved her purple ribbon pin to the bodice of her ballgown. After tonight, she would no longer need such a frock unless Andrew should request her to wear it. How delightful it would feel to have him slide the gown off her shoulders as he sought her breasts. She gazed at the shimmering Kalamazoo River turned silver by the moonlight recalling the June evening when Andrew had met their boat. Now she knew the strength of his arms and his heady scent of leather and green leaves.

When the ferry reached the Saugatuck side, Andrew guided the team to the rally and tied the reins to a hitching post. Ginny wrapped her arms around his neck, and he lifted her from the wagon. She yearned for him to lay her down in his hay mow, but first she would stand with her sisters demanding the right to vote. Sliding her arm in Andrew's elbow, they walked toward the flaming torches and a cloud of women wearing white. She scanned the crowd and spied Anne and the artist from Chicago.

"We shall never stop marching until we can vote!" Mrs. Lewis shouted, and the other women cheered. A few women glanced at Andrew and shrugged their shoulders. Outside the gathering stood a handful of men including a reporter from the local newspaper.

Ginny and Andrew crept through the crowd until they reached Anne in her white dress slashed by a white sash bordered with green and purple. She introduced them to her artist friend, Mr. Anthony, and they shook hands.

"What happened at the ball?" Anne handed Ginny a sash. "For the upcoming march."

"I'll tell you tomorrow." Ginny straightened her spine and listened to the speaker. She belonged here with these strong women who refused to let men and society continue to define their futures. A couple of the women held the hands of their daughters whose faces glowed with wonder. Perhaps Ginny would teach those children and would educate the girls to think. When the rally ended, the women drifted away, and Anne kissed Ginny's cheek.

"Enjoy your evening. I'm ready for bed." Anne nudged Ginny before she and her gentleman strolled back to the hotel.

"Do you want to go home, or would you like to walk along the dunes?" Andrew tucked her arm in his as they stood on the ferry.

"The dunes. Though in this dress…" Ginny ran her palms over the skirt.

"I know of a trail that's not too steep." Andrew grabbed her hand as the ferry docked. "We'll leave the team by that cottage. I deliver firewood to them."

Ginny held up her skirt as the path dipped and rounded a curve before heading up a small rise. The roar of waves sounded closer, and they quickened their steps. At the crest of the dune, Andrew slid an arm around her waist. She drank in the vastness of the lake and the foam flecking the edges of the waves. How fitting to stand next to the man she loved surrounded by the music of the lake.

"I think your purple ribbons made my mother rethink her opinion about women having the right to vote and about other things. She's decided to move to the other side of the state and live near my sisters."

"You'll miss her. I will, too." Ginny rested her head against Andrew's shoulder and sighed, hoping her parents would come to love him, too.

"She believes it would be better if she no longer lived in the farmhouse."

"Oh?" Ginny gazed up at Andrew. "Why is that?" His look displayed his tenderness and his rising desire matched hers.

Andrew swallowed and reached into his pocket. "Would you please marry me and share that house?" He opened his palm and a slim gold ring with three pearls shone in the moonlight. "It was my grandmother's. Without the peach crop I couldn't afford to buy a ring."

Reaching up, Ginny took Andrew's face in her hands. "When Mrs. Rose fitted this gown, she said that after my beau saw me in it, he would propose. All I could think of was how I wanted you to be the one and not William. I would be thrilled to marry you and live in your farmhouse. And to be the keeper of your grandmother's ring."

Andrew slipped on her ring. Standing on his toes, Ginny met his lips and swirled her tongue over the roof of his mouth as his thumbs snuck beneath the ruffle and brushed her breasts. She inhaled as fire swept over her.

"Thank you, my love." Andrew's lips nudged aside the black lace ruffle and he kissed the curve of her bosom. Ginny inhaled and ran her hands down his back. Anne was right about yearning to satisfy and be fulfilled.

"I can't wait for that blanket in the hay mow. Or beneath the peach trees, or in the pasture, or on the dunes."

Andrew nuzzled her neck. "Any time?"

"Anywhere with you."

Epilogue

Golden sassafras and brown oak leaves fluttered to the earth as Andrew's boots clattered on the porch. With his arms outstretched little Jimmy toddled to the door, and Ginny laughed as Andrew swept his child up into the air and his son squealed. Anytime and anywhere had birthed their child one month before their first wedding anniversary. Throughout her pregnancy Andrew had worried about losing her, but after a normal delivery their baby had arrived waving his fists and bellowing. A few weeks later when Ginny had placed Jimmy in her mother's arms the shadow separating them had drifted away. On their wedding day her father had slipped the "paid in full" invoice into Andrew's suitcoat's pocket and for this second anniversary he had ordered them a new John Deere tractor. Claiming how he had bought stock in the tractor company, they had better support it. With Jimmy on his hip, Andrew leaned over and kissed the hollow of her neck where a lucky stone dangled from a ribbon. A purple ribbon sparkled on the bib of her apron.

"Do I smell chicken and dumplings?" He caressed her rounding stomach. "How is our little girl?" When Jimmy squirmed, Andrew set him down and the lad toddled toward his highchair.

"She's eager to meet her Daddy. And yes, chicken and dumplings." Ginny closed her eyes as Andrew's hand drifted behind the bib of her apron. Two years wed and heat still exploded when his fingers unfastened a few buttons.

"Where should we celebrate our anniversary? An evening in the orchard? Or the haymow? Jimmy can sleep on a blanket."

Ginny exhaled Andrew as his fingers wandered, and his mouth moved over hers. Why did he tease her so? Yet over the months, she had discovered ways to entice her husband.

"In that little dip below the sheep pasture." Ginny's lips brushed Andrew's. "At sunset."

The End

Author's Note

Lake Michigan's shimmering blue waves and stunning sand dunes grace the shoreline near Saugatuck, Michigan. Every summer, hundreds of visitors rent cottages, revel in the sunsets, and wander the beach searching for lucky stones, a small round fossil with a hole in the center of the disk. The summer traffic spills over into nearby Douglas and Fennville where I live on an organic fruit farm. Many years ago, I spent the summer as a housekeeper/companion for an elderly woman whose family built one of the first cottages on the Lakeshore and I patterned Ginny's home after that cottage. Shorewood exists a short walk away and is populated by persons much kinder than William and his crowd.

For over a hundred years, the Chicago Art Institute has hosted a summer school at Ox Bow, a cluster of cabins and buildings located in the dunes on the south side of the Kalamazoo River. Ginny's chef, Francis Chapin attended Ox Bow both as a student and later as faculty. Over the years, some of the artists chose to reside in the area and their studios dot the countryside and galleries display their artwork from Saugatuck to Fennville.

When visiting the lakeshore, a ride on the chain ferry, the only one in the United States, is a simple way to touch history and enjoy a method of transportation that Ginny knew. In 1889 the woman I worked for journeyed by the Interurban from Chicago to New Richmond and boated down the Kalamazoo River to Douglas, therefore Ginny travel in that same manner to reach her cottage. During the nineteenth century, fruit farms extended down the Lake Michigan shoreline from the Indiana border to north of Holland, Michigan which is why Andrew entered the story. While the halcyon days of fruit farming have vanished, in places orchards still flourish with apples, peaches, and sweet cherries along with rows of blueberry bushes or acres of grapes for making wine.

While writers tend to work in isolation as they conjure verbal images in their minds, we acknowledge the contributions of our families and writing friends. So, thank you to Suzie Jenkins for asking me to write a novel for the Hot Summer Romance set of books. Thank you to Kay Hubbard for your editing and proof-reading skills. Thank you to my husband, John, for understanding my passion to write. One of my literary quirks is inserting names of friends in my novels as a fun way to recognize their influence in my life and our community. If you see your name here, thank you for being my friend. Because of her contributions to the local Women's March, Garnet Lewis leads the suffragist rally that Ginny attends.

Biography

Joan Donaldson is the author of several picture books and award-winning novels, including the 2010 Friends of American Writers Award for *On Viney's Mountain* that represented the State of Tennessee at the 2010 Nation Book Festival. Her personal essays have appeared in *The Christian Science Monitor* and *Ideals* and have aired on Michigan Public Radio. In 2008, she earned a Master of Fine Arts in Creative Writing from Spalding University. Along with her husband, John, she makes her living growing organic blueberries. With her grandchildren, she enjoys feeding the fish in her pond and tending to her gardens. She is learning old style Irish step dancing, plays Irish and Scottish traditional music on her Celtic harp and sews quilts. Joan is represented by Terrie Wolf of AKA Literary Management.

If you enjoyed this book, please consider leaving a review at Amazon as ratings and reviews promote books and help sales. Thank you.

You can learn more about Joan at www.joandonaldson.com and at her Author's page on Amazon: https://www.amazon.com/~/e/B001K8RCFC

Made in the USA
Monee, IL
12 July 2021